D0015718

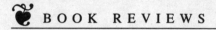

❦ BOOK REVIEWS

Here's what people are saying:

The characterizations of Julie and the minor characters are excellent. Julie is a well-rounded character who undergoes several changes . . . from indecisive dreamer to a determined realist.

from SCHOOL LIBRARY JOURNAL

Teenagers will identify with Julie, her dreams and her aspirations.

from CHILDREN'S BOOK REVIEW SERVICE INC.

ESPECIALLY FOR GIRLS®
Presents

WANTED:

DATE FOR SATURDAY NIGHT

Janet Quin-Harkin

PACER BOOKS
a Member of the Putnam Publishing Group
New York

For my godmother,
Gwladys Rees

This book is a presentation of Especially for Girls®
Weekly Reader Books.

Weekly Reader Books offers book clubs
for children from preschool through high school.

For further information write to:
Weekly Reader Books
4343 Equity Drive
Columbus, Ohio 43228

Edited for Weekly Reader Books
and published by arrangement with
Putnam Publishing Group.

Especially for Girls and Weekly Reader
are trademarks of Field Publications.

Published by Pacer Books,
a member of The Putnam Publishing Group
51 Madison Avenue
New York, New York 10010

Designed by Alice Lee

Library of Congress Cataloging in Publication Data
Quin-Harkin, Janet.
Wanted: date for Saturday night.
Summary: Fifteen-year-old Julie, worried that
she may be the only freshman without a
date for the freshman formal, decides
to impress everyone by appearing at
the dance escorted by a hand-
some college student.
I. Title
PZ7.Q419Wan   1985   [Fic]   84-18909
ISBN 0-399-21150-0
Printed in the United States of America

Chapter One

"**W**HAT'S wrong with me, Gerry?" I asked. It was the first thing I had said all afternoon. Gerry, my best friend, hadn't really noticed because it had been too cold outside to talk—the sort of day where the wind froze your tonsils if you opened your mouth. Then, once we were inside Al's Bettaburger, Gerry's mind had centered totally on her food. Eating was one of Gerry's major hobbies, along with acting and boys. She was good at all three.

Gerry parted her long black hair so that she could stare at me closely.

"Why? Don't you feel good?" she asked. "You look OK to me." Then she went back to attacking her betta-burger. It took a lot to swing Gerry's mind away from food when she was in the middle of serious eating. Only a very cute boy walking past would have done it. The sickening thing was that she still managed to look slim and gorgeous and curved in all the right places in spite of millions of calories a day!

"It's this dumb Freshman Formal," I said.

Gerry finished her burger and gave me her undivided attention. "What about it?" she asked. "I didn't think something like a school dance would matter to you. You're not usually into stuff like that."

"I know," I said, playing with the pickle at the edge of my plate. "Usually I'm not. Usually it wouldn't matter to me one bit whether I went to a school dance or not. But today Caroline Hansen's group was talking about it, and Caroline was saying that *everyone* in the freshman class went to it. If you didn't show up, you were a nobody, a great big zero."

Gerry laughed. She was one of the few people in the world who was not impressed by Caroline Hansen and her group. She didn't seem to care who was popular and who liked her or hated her. Perhaps that was one of the reasons I like her so much–she made her own rules and she wasn't afraid of anything or anybody. "Well, you know what Caroline is like," she said lightly. "Little things like Freshman Formals matter to her."

"So you won't be going either?" I asked.

"Oh, I expect I'll go," she said. "Whoever I'm going out with in a month's time will probably want to go. Besides, I don't often get the chance to dress up in a nice, long, beautiful dress." Another thing about Gerry was that she changed boyfriends as often as she changed her library books. And she never had any problem finding the next one, either–which was another way we were entirely different.

"So Caroline was right," I said. "Everyone else will be going. "I'll be the only freshman not there."

"Then come," Gerry said.

"With whom?"

Gerry shrugged her shoulders. "There are plenty of boys around," she said. "You know boys."

"Nobody I'd want to be seen dead at a formal with," I said. "I don't need to remind you that I haven't had a date in ages."

"There was that Harold or Harvey something," Gerry said. "Didn't you go to the Youth Group Hoedown with him?"

I shuddered. "That definitely did not count as a date. That was a sacrifice. He had sinus problems and was allergic to hay, and the hoedown was filled with bales of the stuff. It is not exactly fun to dance with someone who is honking, wheezing and snorting."

Gerry giggled and almost choked on her French fry. I had to smile too. Looking back on it, it was funny. That seemed to sum up my entire life until now: tragic at the time, and funny when you looked back on it. But never exciting... or romantic.

"I know I'm not the best-looking girl in the school," I said. "And I don't have what you would call a sparkling personality, but I'm not that bad, am I?"

"Of course you're not bad, Julie," Gerry said. "And there is nothing wrong with you, except you live in a dream world half the time. You have this vision of a dream guy who doesn't exist, and you don't have any time for the ordinary guys around who do want to take you on dates."

"But the sorts of guys who ask me out are so blah," I said. "You don't know what it's like. You always get the exciting guys. The ones I get spend the whole evening stuttering and stumbling and blushing and apologizing every time our knees touch by accident."

"Well, shy guys could turn out to be nice, too, if only you'd give them a chance," Gerry said. "You have to face it, kid. You are not in the Russ Thompson league right now, are you?"

Russ Thompson was one of the popular clique, also a basketball star, student council officer and, by coincidence, incredibly gorgeous. He was one of the few people in the school who was allowed to belong to more than one clique. Our small high school was very cliquey. You either had to belong to the popular crowd or be one of the superjocks, the brains, the organics, the techies or the weirdos. Most people gravitated into one of these groups when school began.

"It would be easier if I only belonged somewhere," I said. "But I don't. I mean I'll never be popular or a superjock or a brain. I hope I'll never be an organic..."

"I should hope not," Gerry said, looking horrified. "Think of trading hamburgers for tofu!"

"So where will I ever meet exciting guys?" I demanded.

"I've tried to get you in with the drama techies," Gerry said.

"I know you have," I said. "And I've tried to fit in, too. But I'm not like them. I feel like I'm being overpowered."

Gerry is involved with the drama club. She acts, she directs, she builds sets and sews costumes... anything, as long as it has to do with a play. That's what the techies are—people who work on the technical side of drama. At home her mother yells that Gerry never lifts a finger to help. Her room is a disaster area. Her mother would go into shock if she could see Gerry sweeping stages, mending theater seats, washing curtains. Gerry knows I like to paint so she brought me in to help on the scenery of the last few plays. I enjoyed being part of it—especially painting. It's not often I get to paint a canvas that's twelve feet by ten—but the people made me nervous. I guess people go into theater because they have a lot of confidence. These people, even the ones who just worked backstage, always seemed to be singing loudly, acting out scenes, doing spoofs on commercials and generally clowning around. Of course Gerry was the loudest and funniest, which made me feel at the time that she was not my best friend at all.

"I don't get you sometimes," Gerry said. "One minute you are complaining that you never meet any exciting guys, and then you say exciting guys scare you. What do you want?"

"I don't know," I said, pushing my plate of food away. "Something that doesn't exist, I suppose. But I do want to go to that formal. I don't know why it's so important to me, but it is. Just for once in my life I'd like to make a grand entrance with a great-looking guy and have everybody whisper, 'Who is that?' and they'd answer, 'That is Julie Klein, the person nobody noticed, now blossomed into full beauty.'"

Gerry laughed. "So where are you going to find this fantastic guy?" she asked.

"I wish I knew," I said. I stared out at the castle on the hill, the old Johnson mansion. If only...I thought.

"Hey, aren't you going to finish those French fries?" Gerry asked.

"I'm not hungry," I said. "You finish them if you want to."

"Boy, this really must be serious," Gerry said, "if you're not going to finish your fries."

"I'm not joking. I really want to go to the formal," I said. "It's become very important to me. I want to be part of the fun things that high school is all about. I want to do something that makes everybody else sit up and notice me." I finished my Coke, stood up and threw my scarf around my neck, almost hiding my face. "But the trouble is," I said through the striped wool, "I don't know where to start."

"You could start by coming to a movie with me tonight," Gerry said. "I always seem to meet cute boys outside theaters."

"I don't know if I feel like a movie," I said.

"Oh, come on," Gerry insisted. "My treat. You need cheering up. I haven't seen you so depressed in ages."

"Well, OK," I said hesitantly. "What's playing? You know I don't like scary things."

"Is that today's paper on the seat beside you?" Gerry asked. "Pass it over here and let's see.

I picked up the paper and handed it to her. "That was thoughtful of someone, leaving their paper for us," I said.

"I hate newspapers," Gerry muttered, scrambling furiously through it. So many pages of junk and you can never find anything." She paused and started laughing. "Hey, here's the thing for you."

"What is it?" I asked, trying to peer around the paper. Gerry had a loud laugh and people at other tables were looking at us."

"Remember you just said you didn't know how to start going on dates," Gerry said, spluttering with laughter by now. "Well, how about this: *Wanted: Mature and beautiful girl to share my walks through nature, my music and my life. Respond to 'Hopeful' Box 321.*"

"Very funny," I said, scowling at her. "I may be desperate but I'm not *that* desperate yet!"

"Or how about: *College professor wants to meet woman with brains rather than beauty*," Gerry went on, peeping up over the top of the newspaper. "That should suit you to a T."

I made a face at Gerry, and she laughed even harder.

"It's all very well for you to laugh," I said. "You've never had trouble meeting boys. I bet you even had dates in nursery school."

"As a matter of fact," Gerry said, "there was a little boy with chubby cheeks and lots of blond curls. I remember I used to chase him and kiss him. He used to run and hide every time he saw me coming."

"I can imagine," I said. "You've always had the nerve to do the chasing. But when someone is shy like me ...Actually I can feel for those poor people who put ads in the paper. I bet a person could get so desperate that putting an ad in the paper and signing it 'Hopeful' would seem like a positive step to take."

"Well, you have a whole high school full of boys to work through before you have to start worrying," Gerry said, serious again. "We are surrounded by a tremendous variety of boys every day. It's just a question of finding the right one. I bet there are cute boys who are as shy as you and just dying for a beautiful but shy girl like you to ask them to the formal."

Chapter Two

IF ANYONE bothered to take a good look at me and Gerry it was obvious that we had nothing in common. I was tall and skinny with a thin, little-girl face, big eyes that were my only good feature and hollow cheeks. My grandma always used to say I looked as if I could do with a good meal, and didn't they ever feed me at home. I wasn't ugly or anything, but I was definitely the sort of person you would walk past in the street and not notice. On the other hand, nobody could fail to notice Gerry. She had wonderful thick black hair and flashing eyes. She wore bright colors and outrageous clothes, changing her fashion to match her current boyfriend. She thought nothing of singing or dancing in the street or in the school halls if she felt like it.

Under normal circumstances she and I would probably never have met. But in the middle of sixth grade she moved to the house next door to my family. They asked me to show her around the school. I can't say I was too enthusiastic about it at the time. In the sixth grade I was just beginning to feel the pressure of fitting in with the other kids. And fitting in meant looking like everyone else. We would call each other up before school and find out what our friends were wearing that day before we chose our own outfit. Even in those days Gerry did not look like anyone else. I thought I would die from embarrassment walking beside a girl in a long purple sweater and black fishnet tights. The other kids gave her weird looks for a few days, but she soon had all sorts of friends and the lead in the school play.

Still, I was her best friend. I used to think that maybe she liked being with me because I didn't take the limelight away from her—also because I was quiet and easygoing, and she sometimes needed a break from her own chaotic world. It was not until much later that I realized that maybe she needed me as much as I needed her.

We walked home together every day that she didn't have rehearsal or set building or tryouts or theater painting after school, and we did homework together if she didn't have a date—which certainly cut down the amount of time we saw each other!

"It's a miracle," I said as we walked home the next day. The weather, after the wintry blast of the day before, was now mild, and the wind had the promise of spring at last.

"What is?" Gerry asked, pausing to catch the eye of a cute boy cruising past us in a red Trans Am.

"We are actually walking home together two nights in a row. Something must be wrong with your social life."

"The new play's only at the read-through stage," she said, "and I'm getting bored with Andy. I've kept him almost a month, after all."

"You sound as if you're looking for a good home for him," I said, grinning at her.

"You want him?" she asked quickly. "You can have him for the formal if you like."

"Gerry, I've already told you once," I said. "I want to find my own guy. Besides, Andy is definitely not my type."

"I don't think he's mine either," Gerry said. "Some days I'm not even sure what my type is. I keep hoping that when Mr. Right comes along, I'll know it."

"That's what I keep hoping," I said.

"Well, you won't even get a chance to meet him if you're so picky about dating guys," Gerry said.

"I'm not picky," I said, "it's just that..."

"I know," she said with an exaggerated sigh. "It's just that you're in love with a guy who doesn't exist. I hate to tell you, but handsome men on white horses do not go galloping around twentieth-century Connecticut looking for dragons to slay and maidens to rescue."

Sometimes I wished I had never told Gerry about my dream man. She didn't understand my need for a pretend world where exciting things could happen to me.

As Gerry was talking I glanced across the street, and for a moment I thought I was seeing things. I grabbed Gerry's arm. "Take a look where the florist shop used to be," I whispered. "Am I hallucinating, or is that window full of dragons and unicorns?"

"Oh that," Gerry said calmly. "That must be the new store they were talking about at rehearsal today. You want to go take a look?"

I was already halfway across the street, weaving in

and out of the traffic. A carved, natural wood sign had been hung over the old *E. Lamb Florist*. It said, *Pure Fantasy*. Without waiting for Gerry, I pushed open the door and went inside.

It was like entering a promised land. I was in a store that looked as if it were stocked just for me. There were shelves of stuffed unicorns and dragons, wizards and dwarfs. There were creatures spun out of glass or molded out of metal. There were rainbow mirrors and pictures and jewelry. I wandered around in a trance.

"Can I help you find something?" the pleasant, red-haired woman behind the counter asked.

"Oh, I'm just looking, thank you," I muttered, having remembered that I spent my last money on yesterday's burger.

"Look as much as you want," she said kindly. "And don't forget to tell all your friends about us. We expect you teenagers to be our biggest customers. We're giving away a free poster to our first hundred customers. Here you are."

She handed it to me rolled up. I didn't unroll it until I was halfway home, already walking along our tree-lined street, far from the traffic.

"What's that?" Gerry had said, noticing it for the first time.

"It's a poster they gave me in the store...for being one of the first hundred to come into the store. You want to take a look in case you'd like to run back and get one?"

As I unrolled it, I gasped. "Gerry—look!" I stammered. The poster was a picture of a knight in black armor. He had dark hair that was swept back in the wind and gray, serious eyes. In one hand he held a shining sword, and in the other he held up a shield against a huge enemy whose form could only be guessed at by its fire at the edge of the picture and its shadow falling across him. But he didn't look afraid. He looked calm and at peace with himself—and wonderful. The young man was exactly like the one who haunted my dreams.

Gerry took a look. "Nice," she said, and walked on.

"This is him! The one I've pictured all these years. It's exactly him!" I yelled, grabbing at her coat.

"He's certainly cute," she said, giving the picture a second look. "If he were real, I wouldn't mind meeting him myself."

"Yeah," I said, gazing down at my poster. "Imagine being able to lie in bed, looking at him! I think I'll redo my whole room around him; get rid of all that babyish stuff."

Chapter Three

I FOUND myself thinking more and more about the stupid Freshman Formal. Everyone I passed in the halls seemed to be discussing who they were going with and what they were going to wear. Each day it was harder to make myself think about anything else.

You are an intelligent human being, I told myself very firmly. A formal is not a matter of life and death. It is not even the most important part of your school career. If you don't go, the world will not fall apart. You will not be branded as a failure for life. It is much more important to concentrate on the upcoming math test.

I knew I was talking sense but I couldn't make myself listen. All I could hear was Caroline Hansen's voice, buzzing around inside my head, saying, "Did you notice that Julie Klein was the only girl in the whole class who didn't go to the formal?" I knew that it shouldn't matter what people thought about me, but it did.

I spent all my spare time making lists of any boy who had ever shown interest in me, and I realized that going with most of them would be worse than not going at all. But I could hear Caroline: "Did you see who Julie Klein brought to the formal? I mean, if she's so desperate that she has to go around with such a turkey..."

I was determined that it should be someone special, but I hadn't a clue where I was going to find him. Of course I knew exactly who the perfect boy for me really was. He lived long ago and all I had of him was the poster on my wall. I had an image of him when I first became keen on Dungeons and Dragons. We had all thought up identities for ourselves and invented champions to protect us. I had been a warrior princess and my champion was Damien Dragonslayer, tall and strong with clear gray eyes that seemed to look right into your soul, and a smile that lit up his face. When I started high school, most of the kids got tired of fantasy games. They said they were too mature for such baby things, and their lives suddenly became full of important, serious matters like makeup and steady boyfriends.

I was the one who couldn't let go of that fantasy world. On one of the many occasions when Gerry lost her temper, she said I was scared to face up to the real world. Maybe she was right. All I knew was that the world of my dreams seemed more attractive and exciting than the real life of Julie Klein. In my fantasy world the people on my side didn't ever let me down.

However much I wanted to bring Damien to life and to the formal, I knew that he had to stay on that poster. I was thinking about this in art class and doodling dragons around the edge of my paper when I should have been copying a bowl of fruit.

"Nice dragon," the boy next to me said, making me

jump and turn my attention back to the bananas. "Do you like dragons and that sort of thing?"

"I like drawing them," I said hesitantly.

"Me too," he said. "That must have been a terrific time to have lived, don't you think? I can just imagine myself galloping on a horse and slaying dragons."

I looked up and really noticed him for the first time. He had fair skin to go with his sandy-colored hair. His eyes were light blue, and he had freckles all over his nose. Definitely not the type to go looking for dragons!

"Yes," he went on seriously, "I rather see myself as a dragon slayer."

A brief vision flashed across my mind: a tall figure in black armor, galloping through the forest, his fair hair streaming out behind him in the wind, his eyes flashing blue fire, drawing a shining sword and plunging it into the heart of the huge, scaly beast so that it toppled like a giant tree, crashing and thrashing until it lay still. Then the knight paused to wipe the sweat from his brow, and I saw the freckles on his nose.

No, I thought to myself. I don't think so somehow. The smile had crossed my lips before I could stop it. I think he thought I was laughing at him. He blushed bright pink before looking down at his drawing again.

"Actually, that's a nice thing to think about," I said to him, not wanting to hurt his feelings. But he'd turned back to his work.

I wondered if he would blush as he rescued the maiden. Another of the shy blah types, I thought. Just my luck to be put next to him.

Our art teacher had made us sit alphabetically because she said there were too many "disruptive elements" in the class. He certainly wasn't one of those. I didn't remember ever seeing him before. He probably was too nondescript to be noticed. Just like me, I realized—or like the "me" I was trying to change. His name was Phillip Kaufman. Not a bad name, or even such a bad face, but he was no one to dream about.

When I mentioned him to Gerry on the way home, I surprised myself. She was often interested in details about a boy she hadn't yet dated, but I never figured she'd like him. I don't know why I brought him up.

"Isn't he tall?" she asked.

"Yes, with sandy hair," I said. "And freckles."

"Oh, he's not at all bad," Gerry said. "He knows some of the guys working on the scenery. I've seen him. A little too quiet for my taste, maybe, but..."

"Can you imagine him galloping around killing dragons?" I asked, giggling. "That's what he told me—that he sees himself as a dragon slayer. You're not going to go after him now that it's almost over with Andy, are you?" I asked. I don't even know if I cared.

"No." Gerry smiled. "I'll tell you who is a real hunk in that art class, though," she said. "Gary Abbott. You know—that friend of Russ Thompson."

"Oh, him! The big, dark football player," I said. "He is really cute. But he doesn't even know I exist. He sat behind me for a while but now he's been moved to the front because Mrs. Wagner's put us in alphabetical order—which is why I'm next to quiet Phillip Kaufman."

"You'd better change your name to Aardvark then," Gerry quipped.

I laughed. "Hey, that's not such a bad idea. At least people would remember me then."

"And you'd get to graduate first," Gerry added.

"Not to mention sit next to Gary all year!"

We were still giggling as we walked up the steps into our houses.

"Is that you, Julie?" my mother called, her voice rising above the television in the living room. She would say the same thing every afternoon.

"No, it's a homicidal maniac," I muttered before I yelled back, "Yes, it's me, Mom!" I had been thinking of ways to break the ritual and was trying for a new answer every afternoon. The next step would be for her to ask, "How was your day?"

"How was your day?" she asked.

"Oh, pretty boring... except that the Martians landed on the front lawn and carried the principal into their spaceship," I muttered.

"What did you say? I can't hear you, Julie... the TV is on."

"I said my day was fine, Mom," I called.

"That's good."

The next question would be, "Are you hungry, or can you wait a while?"

"Are you hungry, or can you wait a while?" Correct again.

"I'm starving." There was no point in asking this question. I was starving every afternoon. But she always asked it because she didn't like to get up from her show and she was convinced I would never find any food on my own. "But don't worry, Mom. I'll find my own cookies," I called, going into the kitchen.

She appeared right behind me, just as I knew she would.

"I said I could find them, Mom," I said.

"Oh, but you won't know about the doughnuts I picked up this morning at that new bakery on Lincoln Avenue," she said, reaching into the cabinet and bringing down a fancy bag. She laid the doughnuts neatly on a plate, put out a napkin for me and sat down to watch me eat. This is one of the disadvantages of being an only child. Parents have too much time to spend on you. They diagnose double pneumonia every time you sneeze, and they check you for too much makeup every time you leave the house. I was also just about to find out another disadvantage of being an only child: you have nobody to pass the buck to!

"You'll never guess who called today," she began.

"Michael Jackson has found out where I live?"

"Michael who?" She's way behind the times.

"A singer, Mom. I was just making a joke."

"Oh. Your Aunt Elaine called today. From California. She said they are all fine, and your cousin Danny is really enjoying life at Yale. He's coming down to New York this weekend for some sort of convention—something scientific."

"He's probably discovered a germ to wipe out the entire Earth. He was always such a science nerd," I said. She wasn't listening.

"I told Elaine that naturally he could stay with us and that you would show him around!"

"You did what?" I stammered.

"I said you'd look after him," my mother went on calmly. "He's never actually spent any time in New York City, so you could take him in by train and do some sightseeing."

I stared at her in horror. "You want me to spend a whole weekend with Danny?" I gulped.

My mother looked up and frowned. "He's a very nice boy," she said. "And he'd much rather go sightseeing with you than with old people like us. He's a college boy now. That's closer to your age."

"But Mom—I just remembered, I promised Gerry that I'd go clothes shopping with her on Saturday..."

"Then you'll just have to explain," my mother said calmly. "Family comes first, Julie. Gerry will understand that."

Gerry thought the whole thing was funny.

"You wanted to meet a boy to take to the formal," she said. "Well, here's your chance. A freshman from Yale no less."

"You have not met my cousin Danny," I said bitterly. "Last time I saw him his voice hadn't even changed, and he was almost sixteen. He was a scrawny runt with big round glasses that made him look like an owl, and all he talked about was his bug collection. Do you think that the life cycle of the dung beetle is fascinating conversation?"

"Well, at least you get to go into the city," Gerry said. "I haven't been for ages. Maybe you could dump him at the bug house in the zoo and go clothes shopping at Bloomingdale's? Or at least maybe he likes to eat, and you could go to a really elegant restaurant..."

"If you think it will be that great, you take him," I said. "Or better yet, come with us. It would be OK if you were there."

Gerry ran her fingers through her hair and lifted it

clear of her face. "You know I'd do anything for you," she said. "But I really need new clothes and this weekend is the only time I've got to shop."

"Then come in with us, and you can shop at Bloomies."

"You do not buy army battle dress at Bloomingdale's," she said, "and that is what I plan to wear when I go to this party with Grant, who is going to replace Andy next week. He has the neatest combat jacket that somebody wore in Vietnam!"

"OK. So don't come," I growled. "You'll be sorry when my cousin turns out to have a bunch of his rich and handsome Yale friends with him, and they say, 'What a pity you didn't bring another girl along for one of us.'"

I was always like this with our friendship. I would do any crazy thing Gerry asked me. Why did she always manage not to be there for me when I needed her? That's not completely true. It's just that even though Gerry and I are best friends, share almost all our secrets and have helped each other through a lot of crises over the years, we are very different. I consider myself a very sensitive person when it comes to other people's feelings, but Gerry sometimes doesn't sense when someone feels hurt or needs a friend around. She's not attuned to feelings at times.

And this was one of those times. Gerry didn't see how much I wanted to have her with me on Saturday when I was assigned to the task of "looking after" Danny.

Of course I couldn't stay angry at her for long. I never did. Next day she was calling for me as usual at seven thirty as if everything were fine. I tried to put the weekend out of my mind, but I kept having this vision of Danny producing little boxes of bugs from his pocket all the way around New York.

My mother went into such a frenzy of cleaning and polishing that you'd have thought Prince Charles and Lady Di were expected. On Friday evening my father drove to the station to meet Danny. My mother was nervously muttering that she hoped he still liked pot roast, and I was still trying to think up an escape route. Was it worth falling down stairs and breaking my leg just to avoid a weekend with Danny the bug lover?

"There's the car now," my mother said. A minute later the door opened and my father came in, followed by a tall, good-looking, dark-haired young man. He put down his bag and looked around with a smile. "This place hasn't changed at all, Aunt Helen," he said in a deep, smooth voice. "How have you been?"

"Oh, just fine, thank you, Danny," my mother stammered. I could tell she was as shocked as I was. "And you remember Julie, don't you?"

His gaze went across from my mother to me. His eyes seemed to sparkle as he smiled at me. "Oh sure," he said. "I remember Julie."

Chapter Four

I WAS IN shock all evening. I couldn't stop staring at him, expecting the vision to melt and this skinny little nerd to be sitting there in his place squeaking, "Wanna see this interesting tapeworm?"

My parents didn't seem to find it odd that Danny had suddenly grown about a foot taller and had pulled a quick change worthy of Clark Kent.

"You're looking well, Danny. Are they feeding you at Yale?" was the nearest my mother came to mentioning that he had put on a hundred pounds or so.

"Oh, you know what institutional food is like," he answered with a grin that reminded me of Christopher Reeve. "It doesn't actually taste like anything. The only good-tasting stuff I've had was some grasshoppers we roasted at a biology barbecue..." And he flashed me a look that said clearly, "You thought I was an imposter, didn't you? But only the real Danny would talk about eating roasted grasshoppers when everyone has a mouthful of pot roast."

"Roasted grasshopper? That sounds interesting," my father said. He was noted for his strong stomach. "What did they taste like, Danny?"

"Crunchy and nutty...a bit like potato chips," Danny said.

"Do you go in for that much, eating insects?" my father went on cheerfully. I noticed my mother was only picking at her food, like me.

Danny laughed. "That was only an experiment for world hunger," he said. "Usually I prefer hamburgers. My main interest in life is no longer the insect world, Uncle Harry. In fact I'll probably go into medicine. Is there any more pot roast, Aunt Helen? That was delicious."

Later I helped my mother carry the plates out to the kitchen. "I couldn't believe it was Danny," I told her. "He looks so different. But it's Danny all right!"

She shook her head as she brought her famous strawberry cheesecake out of the freezer. "Everything he says is above my head," she said. "He always did have a great scientific brain. Make sure you don't marry a genius, Julie. Choose someone nice and ordinary, like your father." We were both grinning as we carried in the dessert.

The next morning I half expected Danny to have changed back to his old self. But he was sitting at the breakfast table, eating a huge bowl of cornflakes, looking, if anything, even better.

Definitely a miracle, I thought to myself as I studied him from behind the cornflakes. If Danny can change so dramatically, then almost anything should be possible in the world. Suddenly I found myself wondering– could someone like a Phillip change? Five years older, no more freckles, hair that no longer flopped down into his eyes, and wouldn't that shy, little-boy look change so that...I saw him walking toward me with a new, easy stride. "Hello, Julie," he was saying in a rich, deep voice. "So we meet again after all this time..."

I must be crazy! I told myself severely. Thinking about Phillip Kaufman of all people. Especially when there is Mr. Universe sitting right in front of me! Besides, a miracle could not make me interested in Phillip. I took a last mouthful of cereal and got up. "Come on, Danny," I said. "We'd better get going or we'll miss our train."

As we rode into the city, I found out that Danny had changed in more than looks.

"You were rather quiet at dinner last night," he commented as the train drew out of the station. "Something wrong?"

"No," I stammered. In the bright light of day I was struck again by how incredibly handsome he was and thought what a pity that he was my cousin. It even flashed through my mind to find out what the marriage laws were regarding first cousins, until I pictured myself dusting a shelf full of creepy crawlies and some of them escaping...

"So are you always silent and mysterious these days?" he asked, his eyes teasing me. "You've certainly changed from the little girl who used to come visit us. Remember how you used to scream every time I took out my pet tarantula?"

"Any normal person would have screamed," I commented. I had a vivid memory of those horrible hairy legs creeping down his arm toward me. "You didn't bring it along for company, did you?" I asked nervously.

Danny laughed. "You'll be happy to know that bugs are part of my past," he said. "I don't keep them for company anymore. I've found that girls are a lot more fun, except they don't fit into matchboxes so easily."

I gazed across at him. "You know I wouldn't have recognized you," I said. "I thought you were an imposter until you started talking about eating grasshoppers."

He nodded thoughtfully. "I must have been a miserable little creep," he said. "But around my junior year I discovered that there is more to life than bugs."

"And how did you discover that? Come on—*Confessions of an ex-Bug Addict!*"

He laughed again. I couldn't help staring at where the California sunshine had etched laugh lines around his eyes when he smiled.

"I discovered the hard way," he said. "It was a very painful time, in fact. The moment I started growing taller and working out with weights a bit, all the girls suddenly noticed I existed. I had all the dates I wanted. But I found it wasn't as simple as that. I'd take a girl on a date, and as soon as I started talking about my bug collection, she remembered she had to be home to watch a TV program, or wash her hair, or finish her homework. That's when it dawned on me that not everyone in the world enjoys the same things."

"So now you don't talk about bugs anymore," I said.

He flashed a winning smile. "Bugs are still of interest to me. But actually," he said, "I don't talk much. Period. But to break the ice sometimes, I ask the girl about herself. Girls always trust a guy who asks them questions about themselves. They tell me what a sincere and understanding person I am."

"You're terrible, Danny. I'll go to Yale personally and warn all the girls about you!"

"Actually, I want to know about the person I'm with. Asking questions is a good thing to do. As for the girls, they know me already," he said calmly.

"And my mother said you hadn't changed," I said, shaking my head. "Was she wrong. So much for the shy boy-genius."

"Everybody has to grow up," Danny said, looking at me. "Look at you. You've changed incredibly in the—three years, is it?—since I saw you last."

"I have?" I was surprised.

"Sure you have. You were a skinny little thing, scared of everything and always running back to your Mommie. You used to blush when I spoke to you—when you weren't screaming about my tarantula, that is!"

"And I'm not a skinny, scared little thing anymore?" I asked, blushing in spite of myself.

He looked at me critically. "I'd say you're turning out fine," he said. "If you did something with your hair you'd look very grown-up. You remind me a bit of that model—what's her name? . . . In fact, if you weren't my cousin . . ."

I sneaked a quick look at myself in the train window. The face that looked back at me was not at all bad—good cheekbones, big eyes. If Danny thought I was OK maybe there was hope for me yet!

Chapter Five

IT'S AMAZING what a few words of encouragement
can do for a girl's ego. I sneaked quick looks at myself
in all the store windows down Fifth Avenue and noticed how much better I looked when I stood up
straight and swung my hips. Usually I felt self-con-
scious about being tall and skinny, and I slouched. At
school, if anyone stared at me, I immediately felt there
must be something wrong, and I tried to slink down
the halls as if I were invisible. But next to six-footer
Danny I wasn't too tall. Besides, he had said I looked
like a model. I watched myself walk past Tiffany's and
tried to glide smoothly in my best model's walk.

We paused to look in Tiffany's windows, made jokes
about how we always paid a hundred dollars for a silver paper clip and how we couldn't live without a gold
toothpick with a diamond on top. Then we decided
which ring Danny should give me for my next birthday.
We had settled on a perfect, square-cut emerald, surrounded by diamonds, although Danny had generously
insisted I could choose two if I wanted another. As we
walked away, I noticed an old couple staring at us.
They were so obviously tourists, up from the middle of
Tennessee or North Dakota or somewhere, and they

were looking at us with warm, sentimental smiles on their faces.

"Don't they make a lovely couple?" I heard the wife whisper.

The husband nodded toward us. "You've got a fine young man there, little lady," he said. "You take good care of him now, y'hear?"

We walked on a bit down the street before we collapsed in giggles.

"He really thought we were choosing rings," I said, shaking with laughter. "In Tiffany's of all places, too! Perhaps they hadn't seen the prices!"

"Oh, I don't know," Danny said, trying to stop laughing and look sophisticated. "I guess I must just look like the sort of person who buys his girl a ring in Tiffany's. So where are we going now?"

"I suppose you want to do the usual sight-seeing tour," I said. "Statue of Liberty, Chinatown, Lincoln Center, the museums..."

Danny wrinkled his nose. "Ah, do you think I have to?" he asked. "I mean, see one Statue of Liberty, you've seen them all!"

I started giggling again. "So what do you want to do?" I asked.

"We could always go to the bug house in the zoo," he said. "Nah, just kidding. What I'd really like to do is get the feel of the city. Why don't we just bum around...go to Greenwich Village, Times Square, Central Park, get mugged...You know, all the exciting things you associate with New York City."

Apart from getting mugged, we did all that. We had a

great time browsing through used-book stores and rec-ord shops in the Village. Danny dragged me into some of the outrageous clothes boutiques and pretended that he adored the weirdest clothes, while I tried to keep a straight face. Then, encouraged by his total confidence, I tried on a few outfits I knew I would never dare wear and tried not to crack up over Danny's comments.

Later in the afternoon we bought picnic food and, followed by nothing more dangerous than squirrels and sparrows, walked through the park eating. It was one of those perfect days that sometimes surprise you in New York City and make you think that you'd really like to live there after all. In the park the first spring flowers were beginning to show, and there were hints of new color on bare branches.

"Pretty," Danny said. "I didn't think New York would be this nice. Maybe when I'm a famous heart specialist I'll have an office overlooking the park. What do you want to be, Julie?"

"I don't know," I said. "I haven't found anything I'm good at yet."

"Oh, come on. I bet there's a million things you could do. You looked pretty good modeling those clothes in that boutique."

"I don't think I'd ever have enough confidence to be a model," I said. "My friend Gerry loves people to look at her. I always think that my zipper must be undone or something if people stare."

"That's just a phase you're going through," Danny said. "I remember feeling the same in my mid-teens. You'll grow out of it when you find your niche in life."

"Yes, but when will I ever find that?" I said. "Everyone else in school is already neatly divided into groups, and I'm one of the drifters on the outside."

"You mean there isn't a great love in your life, human or otherwise?" he asked with a smile.

I blushed, even though I fought hard not to.

"Aha!" he said, wagging his finger like Sherlock Holmes. "So there is! All right, young lady. Confess all."

"It's not what you think," I said, still blushing. "It's just that I haven't found the perfect guy. My friend says that I'm really in love with a guy who doesn't exist. I mean, I fantasize..." My voice trailed off in embarrassment.

He smiled at me kindly. "Well, don't look so guilty," he said. "There's nothing terrible about that. Lots of people love to daydream. Just don't let it get in the way of real life, that's all. I have a feeling you'll grow out of it, just like I grew out of the small world of bugs. I didn't turn out too badly, did I?"

"No," I admitted. "You turned out pretty well. I'm amazed."

"So there's hope for you yet. After all, we share some of the same genes. Have faith," he said, giving my shoulder a friendly pat. A sudden wind whipped up litter and leaves, swirled them around and dropped them again. "It's getting a bit cold out here," Danny said.

"I suppose we'd better go home," I said doubtfully. "My mother will start to worry about us if we aren't home soon."

"Do we really have to get home?" Danny asked. "I always think the evening is the best time in the city. It seems like a shame to leave when everyone else is just

8

beginning to have fun. Why don't we call your mom and then go out to a fancy restaurant?"

"That sounds wonderful," I said, "but that will be kind of expensive."

"So?" he said. "How often do I come to New York? And I do spend most of the year studying hard in the library. I deserve a break once in a while, you know. And you deserve a treat for putting up with me all day."

"Oh, I had a great time," I said. "I've enjoyed every minute."

"Even better than the time I showed you my new scorpions?" he said with a grin. "Come on, let's find a phone booth."

"So you can change into Superman?" I quipped, thinking that he didn't need to do any changing.

"So you can phone your mother, dummy," he said, grabbing my hand and darting out through the traffic with me.

He chose a restaurant just off Broadway near Lincoln Center. It had a striped canopy out over the street and no menu or prices outside. I knew his family was not hurting for money. In fact, I remember hearing my father saying to my mother that Aunt Elaine must be loaded, what with the insurance policy and the sale of the shoe company. But it still seemed like a dream to be sitting here with the candlelight and the starched white tablecloths. I didn't actually like the veal in the rich, creamy sauce that I ordered, but the food didn't really matter. Just being the sort of person who sat at candlelight tables with a good-looking boy was the only thing that mattered. And even if that guy was my cousin, and I was only there with him because my parents had insisted, it was still the most special evening I'd spent as far as I could remember.

Danny must have caught the dreamy look on my face. "I bet your boyfriend doesn't bring you to places like this too often," he said smugly.

"I don't actually have a boyfriend right now," I muttered, coming down from my rosy cloud with a bump.

"What happened, did you just break up or something?" he asked.

I played with my fork, drawing lines on the tablecloth. "I guess it's a case of the ones I like don't like me," I said. "My friend Gerry tells me I'm too choosy. I suppose I am."

"And none of the kids at your school measure up to the boys in your dreams, right?" he asked. I looked up, surprised that he had understood. "You wait," he said. "Before high school is out you'll have gotten up enough confidence to go out and enjoy life, and then you'll be fighting off the boys."

"I wish," I said. "The trouble is that I'm still kind of shy. When I meet a boy I really like, I always seem to say something dumb."

"You haven't said anything dumb to me," Danny said.

"But you're different," I said. "You're my cousin. You have to be nice to me or my mother phones your mother to complain."

"You have one problem," Danny said firmly. "And that is that you've got to believe in yourself. I've dated a lot of girls, and I can tell you this—if I had had a boring day with you, I certainly wouldn't have waited around to blow all this money in a restaurant. You'd have gotten a hamburger at McDonald's or we'd have eaten at home with your mother and father."

"Honestly?" I asked, feeling my cheeks glowing.

"Look at this face," he said. "How could you not trust a person who knows the entire life cycle of the dung beetle? Come on—let's hurry before we miss the last train."

We came out of the restaurant to a light drizzle. "We'll have to make a run for the subway," I said, shivering as I turned up my jacket collar.

"Nonsense," Danny said grandly. "People like us who come out of fancy restaurants always go to the station in a taxi."

He stepped forward and waved at a yellow, speeding form. It didn't even slow. We waited a while. A wind joined the drizzle and turned it into stinging rain. Danny came back to join me under the canopy.

"Hey, you're shivering," he said, putting his arm around me and drawing me close to him. "I can't have you catching pneumonia on my account."

It felt wonderful standing there in the warmth of his arms. In fact, I began to hope that a taxi would never come and we could stand like that forever. The rain came down harder and another group of people rushed in under the doorway awning, alternately laughing and complaining about the rain. At that moment a doorman appeared from inside the restaurant with an enormous umbrella.

"Were you waiting for a taxi, sir?" he asked Danny. Then he stepped to the curbside, waved, and magically a yellow blur slowed and swung to the curb.

"Your taxi, sir," he said, holding the umbrella over us.

Danny still had his arm around me as he steered me through the crowd of people toward the cab.

"Excuse me," he said, trying to break up the tight huddle of teenagers in front of us. As they broke apart, I realized for the first time that I knew them. It was Caroline Hansen and Russ and their popular group from school. They recognized me, and, as if they couldn't believe their eyes, they watched as Danny steered me across the sidewalk and helped me into the taxi. I could see them still staring as we sped away.

Chapter Six

"So HOW WAS your weekend with the bug addict?" Gerry asked as we walked to school on Monday morning.

"As you see, I survived," I said bravely, trying to stop the smile from twitching at the edges of my mouth. "But it wasn't easy." I started straight ahead as we walked down the street.

"Look, I'm sorry about letting you down," Gerry said at last. "I felt really bad about it. But you know how much I wanted to make a good impression for Grant, and I didn't have any of the right clothes. I had to do some shopping, didn't I?"

"Oh sure," I said, enjoying for once a position of power over Gerry. Let her feel bad a little longer. Later I might tell her that being alone with Danny was the best thing that ever happened to me and that if she had come, Danny would not even have noticed I existed.

"I understand," I said bravely. "How was your date with the gorgeous Grant?"

Gerry gave a sign which I first took for ecstasy. "To sum it up in one word, boring!" she said. "All he could talk about was cars and car racing and car engines. We went to his friend's party and nobody even danced. They sat around and talked about cars. The only exciting moment in the whole evening was when I fell asleep and slipped off my chair! I tell you, Julie, I'm beginning to think all high school boys are immature! You should have seen these big guys all making racing car noises while they described this stock car race to each other. Your cousin didn't happen to bring any handsome college friends with him, did he?"

"Nope."

"Pity. Do you realize I've worked my way through hundreds of high school guys and haven't found the right one yet? The ones who aren't too immature always want to start a wrestling match in the back seat the minute you go out on a date with them."

"I don't know what you're complaining about," I said. "A least you can get any boy you want. Think of someone like me. I still have to find someone for the formal." As I said this, a crazy picture flashed across my mind—Danny in a white tux walking up the steps beside me. "Pardon me?" Gerry was still talking and I hadn't heard a word she'd said.

"I said we'll have to find somebody for you," Gerry said. "With my connections, it shouldn't be that hard."

"Oh, don't worry about me, Gerry," I said bravely. "I expect I'll survive."

"The right boy will come along some day, I'm sure," she said. "I must run over to the theater and see if that scenery collapsed over the weekend. It was only held together with Scotch tape. See you at lunch, maybe. I might have an extra rehearsal. Bye."

I grinned to myself as she rushed off toward the

theater, leaving me to walk up the front steps alone. If only, I thought dreamily. If only I could persuade Danny to come back for the formal. Imagine Gerry's face when I showed up with him, and Caroline's and everyone's! With a smile on my face I went into the girls' bathroom to brush my hair.

"Well, look who's here," Caroline Hansen said. She was standing at the mirror with Devon, who always looked as if she had stepped straight out of a fashion magazine, and Tracey, who was head cheerleader and looked so much like a cheerleader that she was almost a cartoon. And of course there were the usual hangers-on. All those eyes turned to look at me, and I stood there wishing the floor would open up and swallow me. Caroline broke free of the crowd and walked toward me, her ash-blond hair bouncing around her shoulders, looking more than ever like the teenage Cheryl Tiegs. "Well, aren't you the sly one," she said.

"Me?" I asked. It came out as a little mouse squeak.

Caroline turned to look back at the others and laughed. "Don't you love it the way she plays so innocent? You had everyone fooled, you know, Julie. We all thought you were one of those shy little things who never went anywhere. A real loser. I've never seen you at a party...and now we know why."

"What are you talking about, Car?" a tall, dark girl asked. I recognized her as another cheerleader. Her name was Luanne.

"Tell Lu what we saw on Saturday, Devon," Caroline commanded.

"We had been in the city for the day," Devon said, "and we were just on our way home, very late, when it started to rain. So we ran for shelter in this doorway, and there was a couple standing behind us with their arms around each other. Then the doorman came out to get them a taxi, and they ran across in front of us to get in...and you'll never guess who it was. It was Julie..."

"And the most incredible, good-looking guy," Tracey interrupted. "And they'd just come out of the Fleur de Lis, too."

"So come on, tell us, Julie," Caroline said. "Who is he, where did you find him and how come you've been hiding him from us so long?"

"I haven't been hiding him," I stammered. "He doesn't live around here. He's a freshman at Yale." They were all standing around me, looking interested and impressed. It was the first time in my whole life that people like this had noticed me, that I'd been the center of the "in" group. Were they going to find out that he was only my cousin and that he had only taken me out because my parents had assigned me as his guide for the day?

"Wow, Yale–how about that!" Devon said. "That's real class. Where did you meet him?"

"I've known him a long time," I said. "You see, he's–"

"No wonder she doesn't hang around with any of the creeps at this school," Tracey said, grinning at me. "You wouldn't catch me with Tom if I could have a freshman from Yale...and he looked like that!"

"Does he have any friends, Julie?" Lu asked. "Any lonely, good-looking, rich friends?"

"I don't know," I said. "I'll have to ask him."

"You don't think a guy from Yale would look twice at

you, Lu Becker," Tracey teased. "They're only interested in more mature types—like Julie and me."

"You? Mature?" Devon spluttered. "Who was playing submarines in her bubble bath last week? I bet Julie never plays submarines in her bubble bath."

"Yeah, you know, I always thought you looked like a mature person," Caroline said. "So tell us, when are we going to get to meet... what's his name?"

"It's Danny," I said. "And I don't know when he can get down again. He has to work very hard to keep up his grades."

"But he'll definitely come for the Freshman Formal, won't he?"

"I hope so," I said.

"You must bring him to our party afterwards, over at Russ's house," Caroline said. "I can't wait to meet him. I know you'll—"

The bell for the first period jangled through the tiled bathroom so loudly that I couldn't hear her last words. The group broke up instantly.

In the middle of the chaos Caroline tapped my arm. "If you want, stop by and say hi at lunchtime. We're always in the corner of the cafeteria next to the machines. OK?" Then she ran off, too. It was not until they had all gone that I realized they didn't know that Danny was my cousin.

Chapter Seven

IT'S AMAZING how some days you can't do anything wrong. I haven't had many of them, but Monday was definitely a day like that. I seemed to be the only person who could see what the author was getting at in English. I even found the math test easy. I kept remembering Caroline and her friends standing around me, looking at me as if I were an exciting person and, in the back of my mind, a picture of Danny and me, walking hand in hand into the dance, kept flashing on and off. "That's Julie Klein," everyone would whisper. "She's the one who dates the guy from Yale." And when a mean little voice interrupted, reminding me that he was only my cousin, I wouldn't listen.

I didn't think I would have the nerve to join Caroline's crowd at lunchtime. After all, you can't just change personalities in a few seconds. The real me worried that Caroline hadn't meant what she said. I imagined her cold voice asking, "What are you doing hanging around here?"

But Gerry didn't show up at our usual meeting place by my locker, so I talked myself into just walking through the cafeteria past Caroline's table. If nobody noticed me or said anything, then I wouldn't make a fool of myself.

As it happened, Caroline herself was going back to her table, carrying a tray of food, just as I came through the door. She saw me right away.

"Over here, Julie," she said, giving me a big beaming smile.

I felt my cheeks burning and my heart thumping as I followed her to her table. The faces all looked up, but they were not hostile.

"Everybody, you know Julie," Caroline said. "Julie, do you know everybody?" And she went around the table. Four boys and four girls. A perfect set. I felt awkward, although Devon and Tracey scooted over to make room for me. Tracey even offered me her bag of chips.

"You remember Julie, don't you, Russ?" Caroline asked, giving him her sweetest smile.

"I remember," he said, not too enthusiastically. "She went off in her taxi and didn't offer us a ride."

"Don't be silly, Russ," Tracey bubbled. "How could all of us have squeezed into one taxi! Besides, she wanted to be all alone with *him!*"

"I didn't have a chance to tell you before," Caroline said, very evenly, "but that great-looking guy is a student at Yale. You've heard of the place—it's full of rich and intelligent young men."

"So?" Russ asked, looking amused.

"So I'm just warning you to be on your toes, or I might have to ask Julie to introduce me to one of her Yale friends."

"Ha! That's a laugh," he said, but added, "they only go for mature and intellectual girls, you know."

"Well, Julie's got herself a great guy," Devon said calmly. "And she doesn't come across as mature and intellectual."

"Who knows what Julie's like out of school?" Caroline said, giving me a knowing look. "She's mature and intelligent enough to know that it's not worth dating any of the creeps around here."

"Well, if that's how you feel," Russ said, "I can think of a hundred girls who are all lining up to get my attention."

"Russ Thompson, did anyone ever mention you are totally conceited?" Caroline said, coming around the table to wrestle with him.

I watched them like a spectator at an aquarium. They were all interacting with each other, and I was safely behind the glass wall, not part of what was going on at all. Would I ever feel secure enough with a boy that I could tease him the way Caroline was using me to tease Russ? I couldn't help admiring them. They were all so relaxed in the way they behaved. If only I could stick around them for a while, maybe some of their confidence would rub off on me. But of course, if they found out Danny was only my cousin, only out with me because my mother had volunteered me for the day, and only with his arm around me because I was shivering, then I would be more of a nobody than ever.

There's no reason for them ever to find out, is there? I asked myself, pushing away the uneasy feeling of guilt to the back of my mind.

In art class the teacher announced that several students had been chosen to paint posters to decorate the gym for the formal. The theme was "Carnival in Mexico," and the plan was to decorate the hall with bright posters—scenes from old Mexico. To my amazement and delight, I was one of the people chosen. So was Phillip Kaufman.

"How about that? We're both talented and we didn't even know it," he said, giving me an encouraging smile. "Too bad they won't let us paint dragons. How are you with bulls?"

"I don't know," I said. "I've never tried. Maybe I'll paint mine charging so fast that they'll just be a blur of black."

"Good idea," he said. "The nearest I've ever come to drawing a bull was the cow I drew in kindergarten for an ice cream contest. I won three months of free ice cream, although the cow had udders and legs in the strangest places."

I laughed and the art teacher frowned in our direction as if we were about to turn into a new "disruptive element."

We spent the rest of the period working on one of the posters, and the result was good.

"These paintings are fun, and I think we're doing a great job. Who knows? We might be discovered if any art critics come to the Freshman Formal," Phillip said as we packed up our things and walked toward the exit together.

"Bye, Julie." He turned to leave, then quickly looked back and said, "I really enjoyed today." He waved and walked in the opposite direction.

As I turned toward my locker, I saw Devon and Tracey looking at me with interest.

"Another admirer?" Devon asked.

"Oh, him," I replied, looking down the hall toward Phillip's disappearing back. "He's just a guy from art class."

"He was certainly gazing at you with those big blue eyes," Devon continued. "Hey, you're blushing. Don't tell me you're interested in him?"

"Of course not," I said hastily.

"I should think not," Tracey said, giggling. "I mean, if the guy from Yale found out, he'd be really jealous!" And she broke into a little peal of laughter.

"I tell you who else wouldn't like it," Devon said, looking around as she spoke. "Caroline, that's who."

"She'd think he was too much of a jerk for a friend of hers to be seen with?" I asked, smiling. "Well, she doesn't have to worry about me!"

"No, not that," Devon said, dropping her voice. "She had a crush on him herself."

I looked down the hall. Phillip was disappearing around the corner.

"Caroline had a crush on him?" I shrieked.

"Shhh!" Devon warned. "She might hear you – and she hates to be reminded about it. She really liked him in eighth grade, before she got mixed up with the football crowd. She asked Phillip to go to a dance with her and he turned her down. She's never forgiven him for that. So stay away from him if you want to be friends with Caroline!"

"I had no idea about that," Tracey said breathlessly. "Who would have thought? Caroline and Phillip Kaufman!"

Yes, who would have thought it? I wondered. Caroline was pretty and popular—what had she seen in a guy like Phillip? I'd better take another look at him in art class tomorrow, I thought.

"Well, Julie doesn't need to look at any guy in this school when she has a boyfriend from Yale," Devon said. "I'm dying to hear all about him and how we get to meet his friends!"

"Me too," Tracey said. "I have dance practice this evening, but maybe tomorrow we can all go out for pizza, and you can tell us how you met him."

"Sure," I said. "That would be great."

"I have to run now, Julie," Tracey said. "But I'm glad we're friends. Bye."

Then they hurried off down the hall, leaving me feeling confused.

Chapter Eight

I RAN ALL the way home.

"Is that you, Julie?" my mother called from the living room.

No. It's the new, improved me, with added brighteners, I said to myself as I bounded up the stairs, two at a time. I flung my book bag down on my bed and rushed to look at myself in the bathroom mirror. I half expected to see a different face staring back at me. But the old Julie was still there—same hair, same eyes, same long thin face and hint of freckles on the nose. The sort of face you walked past in the halls and didn't notice—ordinary.

How had I suddenly become the sort of person popular kids were interested in? Just because they had seen me with Danny and thought I was the sort of girl who dated older guys, they decided that they would be interested in knowing me. It didn't make sense. I stared at myself a little harder, then caught my hair in my hand and swept it up into a knot behind my head. Pulled back, my hair made my cheeks look even more hollow and my eyes look larger. Maybe they were right; maybe I did look mature. After all, Danny had said I reminded him of a model.

I ran back into my room and rummaged through a pile of magazines until I found the latest *Seventeen*. The girl on the front had her hair pulled back, too, and big eyes and hollow cheeks. If I could wear that much makeup and the right sort of clothes, it was possible I could look like that, too.

I stood there with my heart hammering, as if I had just discovered King Tut's tomb. I felt that I had just found the key that would open the mystery door for me. I shut my eyes and imagined going to school, dressed like that model, perfectly made up. I could see Gerry staring at me as if she couldn't believe what she was seeing. And I would smile graciously when she told me how pretty I looked. Then I would tell her that I was sorry I couldn't meet her for lunch because Caroline and Russ were waiting...but maybe some other day. Then I would turn and walk away, not slouching at all.

I could just see Caroline's group when I went over to join them at lunch. Gary and Russ would open their eyes wide and stare at me. Devon would look annoyed because she was jealous. Tracey would look at me with admiration. Caroline, as always, would keep her cool. "You look nice today. Is that something your boyfriend at Yale likes?"

Gary would not keep his cool. "Hey, Julie," he would say, "I really go for mature-looking girls like you." And when he asked for a date, I might just go out with him, even though he wasn't even in college yet...

"Julie?" My mother's voice forced me to open my eyes. "Julie, is something wrong?" She was standing there in the doorway with a worried look on her face.

I remembered that I hadn't even said hi when I came in.

"Everything's fine, Mom," I said. "Sorry I rushed up-stairs. I had to look for something in a hurry."

"Did you find it?"

"I hope so," I said, sneaking a look at myself in the mirror. "I really think I did find it."

My mother looked at me as if I were speaking Chi-nese, but she just shrugged her shoulders and, as she turned to go downstairs, said, "I've made brownies, help yourself."

As soon as she was gone I slipped my T-shirt off one shoulder and pulled my hair back into a tight knot again. "So what do you think?" I asked my warrior on the wall. He stared back at me with sad, serious eyes. Then I let down my hair and ran to get the brownies.

Late that evening Gerry called me. She called any evening she could get the phone away from her three brothers and her sister.

"I'm sorry about lunch today," she began before I could say anything. "We had to rehearse that fight scene again. Everybody's swords kept getting tangled up, and we don't want the audience to start laughing when they should be crying, do we? So what did you do for lunch?"

"Oh, I met some kids in the cafeteria and sat with them," I said, trying to keep my voice casual.

"Oh?" Gerry's voice sounded surprised. "Which kids?"

"Oh, just Caroline Hansen and her group."

Gerry giggled. "Ha, ha. Very funny," she said.

"You don't believe me?"

"Oh, come on, Julie," she said. "Why would Caroline

Hansen want to sit with you at lunch? No offense—I mean, I'd rather sit with you any day, but Caroline usually only latches on to somebody when she wants something. Unless they are incredibly rich, or famous or good-looking."

"Well, I guess she must just see my inner beauty and hidden talents," I said. "Oh, and speaking of hidden talents, I was selected to be on the decorating committee for the formal. I've got to paint bullfight posters."

"Terrific," Gerry said. "Maybe that will get everyone to notice you. I can just see it now. Gary Abbott will say, 'Who did that wonderful bull up there?' and everyone will say, 'Julie Klein in your art class.' Then he'll say, 'What a pity her name's not Aardvark, or I could have sat next to her...'"

"You are an idiot," I said laughing. "Actually it looks like I'm stuck with Phillip Kaufman for the posters. We were selected from my art class. Can't you just see the cozy sessions with the two of us working on our posters together?"

"I don't see what's wrong with that," Gerry said. "You could do worse than him."

"I could do better, too," I said. "And I intend to, thank you."

"We shall see," Gerry said mysteriously. "Fate sometimes does strange things."

"What on earth is that supposed to mean?" I asked suspiciously.

"Oh, nothing," she said innocently. "You'll see. By the way, I really called to ask you a favor."

"No! What a surprise!" I said sarcastically. "What is it this time—take your baby-sitting job for you, lend you clothes, lend you money, run a garage sale, clean your closet..."

"Nothing like that," Gerry said. "In fact it's a very nice favor. I got tickets for the Terry Gilbert concert tomorrow night and I don't want to go alone."

"Terry Gilbert?" I asked. "Is he the one who sounds like a young Barry Manilow?"

"That's him. Remember I raved about him last time he was in town?"

"I remember." I could never forget Gerry's raves.

"So will you come with me?" she asked. "You know I hate doing anything on my own."

"You mean the great Geraldine Price cannot find a date for once in her life?" I teased.

"I don't have to spend all my time with boys," she said smoothly. "I have to devote some time to my best friend, too, you know. It's been ages since we did something together, and this guy from drama club sold me the tickets. So what do you say—will you come with me?"

"Sure," I said.

"Terrific," Gerry said and hung up right away instead of gabbing for a couple of hours longer.

Next day I got up early and worked on my hair and makeup. Whatever I did, I couldn't make my hair stay in place like the model's, so I ended up holding it back with two combs. It wasn't a *Seventeen* makeover, but the effect was definitely an improvement on yesterday's hairstyle. I also put on more makeup than I had ever been allowed before in my life and tried to sneak out of the front door without my mother seeing. That was like a mouse trying to sneak by a cat. She pounced out of the kitchen, waving the lunch bag I had forgotten, took one look at my face and nearly fainted dead away.

"Julie Ann Klein, what have you done to your face?" she shrieked.

"Picture day at school," I said quickly. "They told us to wear bright colors so we won't look pale."

"Yes, but surely they didn't tell you to go out looking like a clown," my mother said.

"You know how quickly makeup fades on me, Mom," I said. "It will all be gone by the time I get to school." Then I slipped out the front door before she could drag me back and scrub my face.

At lunchtime Gerry had to rehearse her fight scene again, and I was brave enough to join Caroline and her crowd. Caroline and Tracey seemed pleased to see me. Devon smiled but the smile didn't quite reach her eyes. She was different from the other two. It was hard to tell what she was really thinking, but I got the feeling that she resented my breaking into their group. They didn't include me in their conversation too much, and I was not yet courageous enough to butt in, but it was enough for me just to sit there and let other kids see that I was one of them. What I did notice as I sat there was that my makeup and clothes were still average compared to theirs. They were wearing the latest fashions while I was wearing the same old blue jeans and sweatshirts I had been wearing all my life. I would have to educate my mother gradually.

Caroline managed to get in another little comment

about going with me to Yale one day and meeting handsome college guys. It had the desired effect, and Russ was suitably upset.

"It's OK with me if you want to date boring old men," he said. "Go ahead and try it. You'll wish you had a strong young high school boy again."

Caroline got up and walked around behind Russ. She nuzzled up to him and ran her fingers through his hair. "Oh, some high school guys are OK, I guess," she whispered. "Especially when it comes to getting tickets for the greatest concerts!"

It turned out they were all going to a concert that night as well. "You want to come, Julie?" Caroline asked. "I know there are still tickets for sale, because they said so on WPFK this morning. It's going to be really great—The Vampires and Teen Death are playing."

It flashed through my mind that I could give Gerry an excuse and then go with Caroline's group instead. After all, Gerry had stood me up lots of times if something better showed up. "You do understand, don't you?" she would ask if a guy asked her out on an evening she had promised to spend with me. I would just do the same thing for once in my life. Then I heard her voice: "You know I hate going anywhere on my own."

"I'm sorry," I said with a sigh. "I'd love to come but I already have something to do this evening."

"Not the guy from Yale!" Tracey panted.

"It's a long way from Yale in the middle of the school week," I reminded her.

"Don't tell me you have more than one guy!" Devon said, and I couldn't tell if she was being sarcastic or not.

"No, it's nothing that exciting," I said. "But I can't really get out of it."

"Hey, Car," Russ interrupted, "you know who else is giving a concert tonight—Terry Gilbert!"

I felt my cheeks start to color and wondered if he could read my mind. But he didn't seem to be looking at me at all.

"Terry Gilbert!" Caroline said. "That wimp!"

"Yeah—do you remember that time we went to hear him?" Russ said, starting to laugh. "All those songs about the little butterflies flying around?"

"Don't laugh," Caroline said. "It's not funny. That concert cost me money. I'm not going to forget that in a hurry."

"Yeah, we should have asked for our money back," Russ said, still laughing. "I don't know how he keeps on performing. You'd think everybody would have caught on to how bad he is by now."

"Oh, all the little old ladies in tennis shoes think he's wonderful," Devon chimed in.

"And all the nice boys from the ballet school," Gary interrupted. They burst out laughing. I felt uncomfortable as I walked away.

That evening I decided to wear Gerry's red pants—the ones she had grown out of and traded to me at a garage sale we'd had. I tried them on, more as a joke than anything, and was amazed to find that they actually looked good on me. I walked up and down looking at myself in the mirror. It was almost as if another person were looking back at me...a fine looking person in red pants I had never thought I would wear. They were absolutely skin tight on me and made me realize that perhaps I had good legs after all. I even toyed with the idea of wearing a strapless top that I'd also gotten from Gerry on a trade. Only toyed, though. Then I chose a frilly blouse instead and put my hair back in its combs again.

I don't know why I'm getting all dressed up for a concert with Gerry, I thought. From what the other kids are saying, all the rest of the audience will be Lawrence Welk fans.

Gerry looked delighted when she saw me. "All right!" she said. "How did you know what to wear? That outfit couldn't be more perfect."

"More perfect than what?" I asked.

"For going to a Terry Gilbert concert, what else?"

Gerry had told me that her mother was driving us to the concert, but as I opened the car door, I realized that it wasn't Gerry's mother behind the wheel and that we were not alone. A guy was sitting in the driver's seat.

"You know Rod, don't you?" she said evenly. "He's the one who gets killed and falls off the balcony in the play."

"Hi," Rod said, giving me an easy wave.

"Hi," I said flatly. I grabbed Gerry's arm as she was about to get into the car. "I thought you said you wanted an evening with your best friend," I hissed between my teeth. "I do not want to tag along on one of your dates, thank you."

"Oh, you won't have to tag," Gerry said brightly. "I really asked you to make up a foursome. Rod wanted to bring a friend, so I said I'd bring you as well. Come on, get in. You're going to make us late."

She almost pushed me into the back seat and I practically fell onto the person sitting there.

"Hi, Julie," said a voice that I recognized, even in the darkness, as Phillip Kaufman's.

Chapter Nine

By THE END OF the evening, I felt as if I were about to explode. I don't know how many times I looked at my watch, hoping and praying that Terry Gilbert would stop singing. It all seemed like one horrible, drawn-out nightmare.

To begin with, Phillip made several attempts at conversation, all of which I had cut short. I knew I was not behaving very well, but I didn't care. He wasn't the right guy for me, I felt sure. When I took a good look at him, I realized he'd *never* turn into someone like Danny. Most of all, I did not want to give him the idea that I had arranged this evening because I wanted to know him better. And another thing: I remembered quite clearly what Devon had said about Caroline and Phillip. If she ever found out that we had gone on a date together, I could count myself out of her popular group for good!

Not that Phillip seemed too thrilled about sitting next to me. He seemed uncomfortable and wriggled around in his seat as much as I did. He asked me a few questions about myself, but finally got quiet. The evening wore on, with Rod and Gerry clowning around loudly, and Phillip and me looking embarrassed and communicating in cave-person grunts. On any other occasion I think I would have enjoyed listening to Terry Gilbert. He sang emotional songs in a deep, thoughtful voice. But I was angry at the whole world for being put through such embarrassment.

"Well, what do you think of him?" Gerry asked at the intermission.

"I think he's a wimp," I said. "I mean, you can only have so many songs about little butterflies flitting around, can't you?"

"I think he's pretty good," Phillip countered. "I really liked that one about the girl waiting for a letter from the soldier."

"Oh, really? You would," I said, slightly disgusted, then buried myself in my program. After that we hardly spoke all evening. I kept looking from Gerry to Phillip to Rod and thinking how immature they were and how much fun it had been with Danny. Maybe Phillip had tried to ask me about myself, just as Danny had, but he'd never be mature and appealing to me. He was just a freshman in high school.

I refused the boys' invitation for us to come to Rod's house for a hot drink after the concert, saying I still had a ton of homework to do.

"So what's been eating you?" Gerry demanded as we stood in front of her house. "I just can't understand you. I thought you and Phil would really hit it off."

"You fixed this whole thing up, didn't you?" I stammered, half choking over the words. "I hope you're satisfied. I nearly died of embarrassment."

"What are you talking about?" Gerry asked. "I invited

Phil along because he likes all the things you like, and he's kind of shy like you."

"How many times have I told you not to try to run my life?" I snapped. "I don't care how nice you think Phillip Kaufman is and how much you think we have in common. I do not want to date him. He is not my type at all! He is totally immature and wishy-washy."

"Well, look who's talking," Gerry said. "At least he was a lot of fun until you put a damper on everything and became almost rude."

"I did not," I said. "He obviously is not interested and was not thrilled about getting stuck with me either."

"I didn't get that impression until you started being sulky towards him," Gerry said icily. "You might have made a bit more of an effort to be pleasant to everyone. So what if I did set this up? You really want to go to the formal. Well, I don't know where you think you are going to find a date if you never even speak to boys. I was just helping out, that's all. And it cost me a bundle to get tickets."

"I'll pay you back," I snapped. "And in the future, don't try out your charity work on me. I don't need it."

"Oh, come on, Julie. You wanted to meet boys. There were two perfectly good boys with us this evening, and all you did was turn them off."

"Don't think I can't get a boy of my own just because I'm a little more choosy than you!"

"I'd call it scared."

"Well, I'd call it choosy! I don't happen to chase after every boy that comes my way, like you do."

"For your information, I do not do the chasing! Boys are just naturally attracted to me! And if you are so choosy, just where are you going to find a date for the formal?"

"As a matter of fact, I already have one," I said. "A very good-looking college boy. Luckily, I discovered where I really belong in life. I belong among people who are more mature than high school kids. Mature people find me interesting. And attractive, too."

"Well, in that case," Gerry said slowly, "I guess you'd better stick to your mature people. I wouldn't want you to get bored with me and my juvenile friends!"

I knew I ought to tell Gerry that I was acting dumb and that I really needed her as a friend. But I couldn't do it.

"Bye," I said.

"Bye," Gerry said. "I'll see you at the formal. I can't wait to meet your mature and good-looking date."

I was shaking when I went up to my room. My legs would hardly carry me and I seemed to have forgotten how to breathe. So what? I said firmly to myself. I don't need her. She's not a great best friend, anyway. She only fits me in when she's not busy with her stupid drama club or her dates. I'll be much better off with Caroline and Tracey. Boy, I can just see Gerry's face when I show up with the popular group. I bet she'll turn green! And when she sees me at the formal with Danny...I'll show her who can get boys! As for Phillip Kaufman, he's a freshman who'll never be my dream boy. Who cares if he likes what I like right now? I pushed the picture of his face from my mind and went to sleep.

Chapter Ten

NEXT MORNING I left for school without waiting for Gerry. We had had fights before, of course. Gerry was famous for her quick temper and had exploded on many occasions. Usually, by the next day she had forgotten all about it and showed up, sure that I would forgive and forget as easily as she had. The truth was that I had never forgotten that easily. I always carried the hurt of her insults around for weeks, but I never had the courage to tell her. Also, I was scared of losing my best friend.

But this time was different. This time I was as angry as she was, maybe even angrier. This time I had other friends waiting for me, and this time she was going to learn that she couldn't walk all over me. I was not going to be her doormat anymore!

I was halfway to school when she caught up with me, running hard.

"Hey, Julie, wait up!" I could hear her way down the block. The clatter of her heels sounded like a cavalry charge. She drew up beside me, panting. "What was the big idea, running off without me?" she asked.

I turned to her coldly. "Don't tell me that your memory is so short that you've already forgotten about last night."

"Oh, come on," she said. "So we had a fight. We both said a lot of dumb things. But it's over now. It's not worth spoiling our friendship by fighting over a boy, is it?"

"It's not a boy, Gerry," I said, noticing the sick feeling that always came into my stomach when I fought with anyone. "It's the principle of the thing. You just won't learn that I want to lead my own life! I've got a mother and father who have nothing better to do than guide my every footstep and worry every time I sneeze."

"But you said you wanted to go to the formal more than anything," Gerry said, looking uncertain of herself for the first time since we met. "I didn't see where you were ever going to meet a boy. You are so totally naive. You always fall for the ones that will never even notice you and turn your back on all the ordinary ones."

"But I don't want a boy if I have to let someone else find him for me," I said. "Can't you get that into your thick head?"

"OK, Miss Popularity. Find your own date, then," Gerry said, half joking and half annoyed. "But if you don't give nice guys a chance, I really think you better advertise soon!"

We walked on together in silence, Gerry's heels clattering, my sneakers making no sound. I began to feel more and more guilty. I didn't really see why Gerry should try to run my life and why I should feel guilty because I told her to butt out of it, but I did. My mother had done a good job of bringing me up with a generous helping of guilt. I worried if I struck out at softball because I had let my team down. I worried about hurting other people's feelings. I even worried if I didn't like the food my mother cooked sometimes. I was already carrying around a large load of guilt because I had lied about Danny. I didn't think I had room for more guilt about hurting Gerry's feelings.

I swallowed hard. "Oh, look," I said. "I know you wanted to help. But from now on, don't help me anymore. I'm a big girl now."

"OK," she said, uncharacteristically quietly. "Only don't come running to me the day before the formal because you are desperate."

"I won't," I said. "Actually I have a pretty good idea who I am going to take."

"Not the college boy bit again," she said, tossing back her hair. "High school guys are really nice, if you'd give them half a chance."

"You don't believe me about that college guy, do you?" I asked. "You also don't believe that Caroline Hansen could possibly want me to have lunch with her. You don't believe that anything fantastic can happen to me. I'm just your sidekick—good old Julie who's always there when needed. Well, I may just surprise you, Geraldine Price. You might wake up one morning and find that I don't need you around anymore."

Then I walked ahead of her and ran up the steps without looking back.

Now I *have* to get Danny to come, I thought. I'll call him tonight.

All day long I planned just what I was going to say

to him. "Hi, Danny, I was wondering if you'd like to come to our Freshman Formal that's coming up?" No, that was too casual. He might just think I was being polite and asking him. "Danny, I'm dying to go to the Freshman Formal, and I won't be able to unless you are my escort." No, that sounded as if I were desperate. Why was this so difficult? After all, the guy was my cousin. I remembered him before he turned into Superman. And that day in New York, he really seemed like a person who would understand. Surely he'd come if I explained how much being seen with him had done for my image and how it would be the greatest thing that ever happened to me!

Tracey and Caroline stopped by my locker at lunchtime and invited me to the diner with them after school. I kept hoping that Gerry would walk past while they were there. I'd love to have tossed off a casual "Oh hi, Gerry" as she passed. But she didn't come. I guess she was over at her precious rehearsal again.

The diner was famous for its terrific homemade ice cream. Normally I would not have chosen to eat ice cream on a day when the temperature was just above freezing, but I was not dumb enough to turn down a chance to be with Caroline and Tracey. Devon didn't come with us. She claimed she had a lot of homework, but again I got the feeling that she resented my coming into the group. We each bought hot-fudge sundaes and chose a table way in the corner.

"OK, Julie," Caroline said after we had taken off the initial pangs of hunger. "Tell us all about it. We're dying to know."

"About what?" I asked cautiously.

"Where you met him, of course."

"Oh, that," I said, quickly fishing around for ideas. "Through my parents, actually."

"Wow," Tracey said, looking at me admiringly through those big blue eyes. "Do your parents have something to do with Yale?"

I laughed. "Hardly. My father works for a bank. Very boring."

"So how did they know Danny?" Tracey persisted.

"Oh, he's the son of someone they know on the West Coast. He was told to look them up when he came to college out here. He came to our house, and then he invited me out." At least I hadn't had to tell any lies yet. My nose was not about to grow!

Caroline looked at me critically. "You mean right there, over dinner with your parents?" The look said clearly, "Why would a Yale man find you so instantly fascinating?"

Again truth was better than fiction. "I think the first time he did it to please my parents," I said. "Also, he was very new to the East Coast. But when we went out, we really hit it off together."

"I should say so," Caroline said. "I mean, a guy would have to think a lot of you to want to take you to the Fleur de Lis."

"His family is pretty rich," I said. "He's used to places like that."

"I can't wait to see the corsage he buys you," Tracey said, shaking her head so that her golden curls all bounced. "What color is your dress going to be?"

"I don't know," I said. "I haven't started shopping yet."

"Oh, you should," she said, looking worried. "All the

best dresses get snapped up around prom season."

"What are you wearing, Trace?" Caroline asked. "That same dress you wore to the winter dance?"

Tracey wrinkled her nose. "Unless I can get my father to cough up some more money. But he's being so difficult. You should have seen him blow his top when he found out how much the winter one cost. I really like it, but I don't really want to wear it twice."

Caroline nodded. "You can't wear the same dress to two dances," she said. "Everyone would notice."

"So you're not wearing the silver one again?" Tracey asked.

"That old thing?" Caroline said. "I already threw that into Mom's goodwill box. That made me look like a little girl. I think I'm old enough for something slinky this time!"

I gazed up at the sausages at the front counter and pictured myself arriving in something slinky. Danny would be in his white tux, of course. Perhaps I could wear a strapless white dress, slit up the side, Chinese style, topped by Danny's corsage of orchids.

"Maybe we can all go shopping together pretty soon," Tracey suggested. "I love going shopping in the city."

"And let's get together the afternoon of the formal and all do each other's hair and nails," Caroline suggested. "I'm dying to do Julie's hair. It would look so good all swept up with little curls at the back and maybe flowers in it."

"Won't you have to help Russ get ready for the party?" Tracey asked.

"There's not much to do," Caroline said. "His mom's having it catered. She said it would be too much for just her."

"Oh great—I love catered food. Don't you, Julie?" Tracey said.

I didn't want to admit that I'd never been to a catered party, except a family wedding, so I nodded and dug into my ice cream.

"The party will be more fun than the dance, I think," Caroline said, turning to me. "You'll love it, Julie. And everyone will be so anxious to meet Danny. You'll have to hang on to him tightly or we'll all steal him away!"

A picture flashed across my mind...Danny and me standing in the middle of the group, being witty and mature. Everyone was laughing at Danny's jokes. "You're so lucky, Julie," Tracey would whisper. "I know," I would say, snuggling up to Danny's white sleeve. He would look down and smile at me. "Great party, kid," he would say, "but getting a little crowded. Why don't you and I get away from the crowd for a while..."

Hey, stop, I said firmly to myself. This was terrible. I was already beginning to believe my own lies. Danny thinks of you as a cousin, nothing more. Remember that, I told myself. If he comes to the formal it will only be as a favor. Not because he is interested in you.

Which reminded me, sharply, that I didn't even know yet whether he would come. Maybe he wouldn't want to be seen dead with high school kids. "I'd better go," I said, getting up. "It was fun to be with you, but I promised Danny I'd call him this evening."

It was pretty late before I finally got up the courage to call him.

"Is that you on the phone, Julie?" my mother called from the living room.

"Yes, Mom," I said, closing the door in case she came out to listen to my conversation.

"Who are you calling, Julie?"

"Just Danny, Mom. He asked me to call him about something."

"Well, don't talk too long. It's long distance," she yelled back.

The phone rang about six times before anyone answered it.

"Danny?" the deep voice on the other end of the line repeated. I could hear music going on and loud male laughter in the background. "Hey Danny!" the voice yelled. "Shut up for a minute, you guys, will you! Go tell Danny there's another girl on the phone for him!" And he laughed as he said it, as if he had made a joke.

Danny's voice, in contrast, sounded suspicious, as if he couldn't imagine who the other girl could be.

"Hello?"

"Danny, this is Julie."

"Julie?" Still suspicious.

"Your cousin...remember me?"

"Oh—Julie!" Big sigh of relief. "What on earth are you calling about? Is everything OK at home?"

"Oh, sure. I called because...congratulations—you have won a fun-filled evening at my Freshman Formal!"

I couldn't believe that's what came out of my mouth. Why did I go and say a dumb thing like that?

"I've *what*?"

"What I wanted to say was...I'd really like it if you

could come down for my Freshman Formal on the eighteenth of next month."

"It's nice of you to ask me, Julie, but don't you think I'm a bit old for that sort of thing?"

"Oh no. My friends are very sophisticated and mature. You'd have a good time. Honestly."

He laughed. "You sound like you really want me to come."

"I do," I confessed. "It will be like the end of the world if you don't come."

"That bad, eh?"

"I know it sounds dumb, Danny," I said, "but I'll tell you the truth. Some of the most popular kids at school saw us together coming out of the restaurant in New York City and you've no idea what that's done for my image around school. If I could take you to the formal, I'd be somebody people admired."

"I take it you didn't mention to them I was your cousin," he said.

"I tried to, but..." I trailed off.

"But to pass me off as your date would be phony, Julie. You must know that."

"I do know it," I said. "But I also know that it's my one chance to make an impression on the kids at school. Perhaps you don't remember what it's like in high school. If you're in with the in-crowd, then everything's fine."

"I remember very well," he said. "Is that what you really want? To be in with the in-crowd on any terms?"

"I want it very much," I said. "If you come, it would be the biggest favor in the world, Danny."

"If it really means that much to you," he said slowly, "I'll try to make it."

"Oh, you will?" I let out a shriek worthy of Gerry at her best. "That's terrific!!!"

"What date did you say?" I could hear the rustling of pages.

"The eighteenth. Saturday."

More rustling. Then a pause.

"Julie, I'm sorry," he said quietly. "You couldn't have picked a worse date. That's right in the middle of finals. I have to study that whole weekend. I have an exam the following Monday."

"Wouldn't a break do you good?" I asked. I could hear my voice trembling.

"I really need all of that weekend to study," he said. "I have to keep up my grades, and I've got so much material to get through you wouldn't believe it. I'm really sorry, Julie. I would come if I could. But I can't. I'm not trying to make an excuse. I really can't come."

There was a pause because I couldn't think of anything to say. I heard Danny's name in the background, above the rock music.

"Julie," he said quietly, "I have to go, OK? Why don't you look around your school? I bet there are hundreds of really nice guys who'd like to take you, and you'd have just as good a time with them."

"Sure," I said, swallowing back the sob. "Well, thanks anyway, Danny."

I hung up the phone and walked up the stairs slowly, one at a time. Then I sat on the edge of my bed and stared out the window. It had been raining and the streetlights twinkled in puddles like stars.

"That's it," I said. "The end of everything. Now everyone will laugh at me." I could just hear Gerry's voice now: "So where is this super-cute college guy, Julie? Or are you dating the invisible man tonight?"

I got up and paced my room like a caged tiger. I have got to get a date for the formal, I told myself. A very special date. I am going to get one... if it's the last thing I do!

Chapter Eleven

I DIDN'T sleep well at all that night. I lay on my bed and watched the branches dancing in front of the streetlight, throwing shadows like skeletons across my white wall. I had just drifted off to an uneasy dream in which I was running down a tunnel, trying to catch a dark figure who kept walking farther and farther away from me until he was almost invisible.

"No, come back. Don't go. Please don't go!" I begged. The tunnel walls echoed my voice until it jangled through my head like a million bells. I woke up sweating and realized that the telephone was ringing downstairs. Nobody else seemed in a hurry to answer it, so I pulled on my robe and staggered down. A tiny glimmer of hope whispered that Danny had changed his mind about the formal. He felt so bad about letting me down that he was going to come, even if he missed a day's studying.

But it was only Gerry. She sounded cheerful, as if it were breakfast time. "Hi, did I wake you?" she asked brightly. "I know it's late but my brother has a new girlfriend, and I couldn't get him off the phone for two hours."

I glanced across at the grandfather clock. Eleven thirty.

"Yes, you woke me," I said before I remembered that we were hardly on speaking terms. "But I was having a bad dream anyway."

"Well, I've been thinking about it all evening, and I decided I had to call you and tell you what I thought," she said. "So if I woke you up, it's for your own good."

"What are you babbling on about?"

"First of all, I want to apologize for what I said about you not knowing Caroline Hansen. I don't know why she made friends with you, but I went past the diner today and there you were, you and Caroline and Tracey, all with your heads together, trading secrets."

"Is there anything wrong with that?" I asked frostily.

"Nothing," Gerry said. "I'm very glad for you that you've been invited into that group. I guess that means you've finally made it in high school. But I'm your friend, and I care about you. I've been worrying about this all evening."

"About what?"

"You and Caroline Hansen's group," she said. "They are not the right people for you, Julie. You don't belong with them."

"And why not?"

"Because you're not like them," she said. "Caroline is wonderful if you stay on her good side. But you try doing something she doesn't like, and you'll find out. You're much too sensitive to be hurt by people like that, Julie. It's just not worth it to be friends with them for a while. They must be using you for a reason, but when that reason is done with, they'll drop you flat."

"I think I get the picture," I said coldly. "You are jealous, aren't you? You liked me as a best friend because

I didn't threaten you. I was always there in the background, a nice quiet person you could turn back to when there was nothing better around. But now that I'm with Caroline and her group, you see that I might be getting popular, too, and that hurts your pride."

"Don't be dumb," Gerry said. "I don't care who you are friends with. But I think you should think it over very carefully before you choose to be friends with Caroline."

"Caroline is fun," I said. "What's more, she has time for me, which is more than you do. I'm tired of playing second fiddle to rehearsals and half the boys in the county."

"OK, if that's the way you feel. Do what you think is best, then," Gerry said. "Choose your own friends."

"I will," I said. "And I'm beginning to think that you might not be one of them anymore. Perhaps I've outgrown you, Geraldine Price. I don't need to hang around waiting to do something with you anymore."

"In that case there's nothing more to say," Gerry said. There was a click, and the line went dead. I went back upstairs, gripping the banister to steady myself. It wasn't until I was in bed again that I realized I wouldn't have Caroline for a friend much longer. Now that there was no Danny, there was nothing to make her interested in me. Unless I could find a boy to replace him!

Next morning, I woke up absolutely determined to find myself a date for the formal. Only I wasn't sure where to start!

I guess that as an only child I have grown up a bit

spoiled. I don't mean that my parents run out and buy me something every time I want it, but it's pretty easy to get your own way when you're an only child. Gerry, for example, has to fight to get the phone in the evenings, or to get the last cookie. I never really have to fight to get anything in my life. If I ask for lasagna for dinner, we have lasagna for dinner. If I want to watch a program on TV, I just switch over to it. This makes for a relatively easy life, but it doesn't help you grow up tough enough for the real world.

There was only one time in my life when I ever felt strongly enough about something to get my own way. In kindergarten, when we were doing a play about the wonders of nature, I desperately wanted to be a butterfly, but Mrs. Kolter made me a frog instead. I happened to hate frogs and knew that there was no way I would hop around the stage being slimy and gross, while other girls got to wear wings and be butterflies. So I had the most terrific tantrum, and I actually held my breath until I turned blue and passed out. That scared Mrs. Kolter so much that she had to say I could be a butterfly.

I didn't think this method would work with boys. I couldn't see going up to a cute guy and saying, "If you don't go on a date with me, I'll hold my breath until I turn blue!" My problem was I couldn't think of anything I could say or do to make the right sort of guy notice me.

I wished I could have been more like Gerry. She knew how to get what she wanted. But Gerry was not my best friend anymore. I had made sure of that. I had been upset about Danny and said a lot of dumb things. I didn't think she'd forgive me in a hurry this time.

It would have been so easy to call her and say, "Gerry, you've got to help me," and she'd come right over and we'd laugh together over crazy schemes. On my own it didn't seem like much fun. It seemed hopeless. How does a girl who can't even get any of the cutest guys in school to notice her go out and find herself an ideal man? Short of standing outside a supermarket and lassoing one while he was busy with a shopping cart, I didn't have any brilliant ideas.

I got dressed and went out for a walk, half hoping, I think, that Gerry would be outside and that we would start talking again. It was a blustery day. Clouds raced crazily across the sky as if something terrible were after them. The wind tugged at my hair, snatched my breath away and got down inside my jacket. Normally I would not have gone out walking on a day like this. But today the weather seemed to match my mood. It was an urgent sort of day. A day for getting things done.

I hadn't a clue where I was going or what I was doing. I just walked. I passed our school, empty and deserted with bits of trash flying around in the front yard. I passed the center of town and kept going. Crazy ideas were flying around inside my head. What if I phoned an escort service and hired a guy to come with me? Unfortunately I had less than twenty dollars in the world at the moment, and I didn't think they'd have too many guys you could rent for that little. And if they did, I knew that I wouldn't want to be seen with one of them! I thought of cruising around the library, bookstores, parks, movie theaters, picking out the right sort of guy, going up to him and saying, "I know this sounds crazy, but would you do me a big favor?" But I knew that I would never have the nerve to do something like that. Gerry would do that, but not me. Even if I got as far as opening my mouth, I wouldn't be able to make a sound come out.

I kept on walking up toward the community college. It was a long hill, and I was out of breath by the time I got to the top. I stood there panting, looking at the town lying comfortably below me with smoke curling up from some chimneys, and windows glinting when the sun peeped from behind a cloud. Up here I felt like the only person in the world. There were a few cars in the college parking lot, but no students coming in or out.

Why couldn't this be Yale instead of the community college? I thought, staring at its ugly brick front with its pseudo-Greek pillars and archway. At least Danny might have been able to find me one of his less studious friends.

I crossed the parking lot and headed toward the main building. But maybe there are some cute guys who go to college here, I thought, watching the pigeons land on the archway, then take off again with a sound like flapping paper. How would I meet them? I asked myself.

On impulse I went up the steps and in through the big double doors. The hallway inside didn't look much different from our school. It had water fountains and bulletin boards and dirty green paint. I walked toward one of the bulletin boards. They certainly were different from the ones in our school. We just had announcements about sports teams and tryouts for plays and scholarships. Here you could put up any old notice you liked. *Wanted: Third student to share apt. with two non-smokers. Can be male or female... Share through meditation... Moped for sale... Second person to share expenses on ski trip... Therapy... Massage...* There didn't seem to be anything you couldn't put up a notice about here.

I walked on down the hall. Most of the classrooms were deserted. I passed the empty art room, its door open and the smell of oil paint creeping out into the hall. If only I could have joined an art course, I thought. That's something I'm halfway good at. I imagined myself sitting in the art class next to a tall, serious young man with heavy-framed glasses. He'd look across at the tree I was drawing.

"That's pretty good," he'd say. "You have a real talent for trees."

"Thank you," I would answer.

"I can never get the hang of them," he would sigh. "Mine always look like a bunch of toothpicks stuck together."

"Oh, it's not hard," I would answer. "It's just a question of knowing the basic shape of the type of tree you are drawing. I'd be happy to help you sometime."

"Oh, would you really? That would be terrific," he would say, a smile lighting up his serious face. "Maybe we could go out for pizza one night soon, if you're not too busy."

"I'm sure I can find a free evening," I would say, smiling back at him.

I hadn't noticed where I had been walking and finally heard the murmur of voices. The arrow on the wall said "Student Center." Surely all I had to do was sit in there long enough and I'd meet people.

I pushed open the door and went in. Several groups were sitting together talking. One group had a stereo cassette player on the table in the middle and moved in time to music I could barely hear. Over in an armchair a dark-haired boy with heavy-framed glasses was sitting alone reading.

I couldn't believe my luck. I wandered over and sat down in the next chair, grabbing a magazine from the table. For a while we read in silence while I practiced all sorts of dumb things to say to him. I tried to remember every one of Gerry's opening lines to strange men, but they all sounded wrong coming from me. I stared hard at the pages of *Motor Mechanic*, and transmissions swam before my eyes while I thought what I could possibly say.

I jumped a mile when the guy leaned across and touched my arm. "Excuse me," he said with a wonderful smile, "but do you know what time it is?" I gazed at him like an open-mouthed idiot. Wonderful. Ask the time. Why didn't I think of that?

I looked at my watch. "It's 10:20."

"Oh, great. Thanks a lot," he said, going back to his book. After a while he looked up at me again. "Are you waiting for someone, too?" he asked.

"Me? Why?" I stammered.

"Because you've been staring at the same page of that auto magazine for ten minutes, and I bet you're not the least bit interested in torques!"

Before I could answer this, a girl came running in. Her hair was so long it flew out behind her like a veil, in the palest gold. Even in her old parka and jeans she managed to look beautiful.

"Jason," she called, waving in our direction. "Did I keep you waiting long?"

The boy rose to his feet. "Let's just say that I've read *War and Peace* twice," he said, giving me a wink.

"Oh, I'm so sorry," she said. "But my car wouldn't start again. I had to call Triple A."

"You should have called *her*," he said, pointing down at me. "She's the expert. Nice talking to you. Bye." He gave me a friendly wave, slipped his arm around her, and they walked off.

I sat there for another hour, watching people come and go, but always in twos or threes, before I decided I was wasting my time. I would never meet a college guy this way. And I couldn't think of any other way. Just go home and admit defeat.

I walked back through the empty halls, hearing my feet echoing. From behind a closed door came the murmur of voices. An orchestra was playing somewhere far off. It was like walking through a dream.

I glanced at the notices as I went past. One was beautifully lettered in calligraphy and bordered with flowers. It caught my eye because it was so attractive. But the moment I looked at it, the message caught my eye even more. *The Trading Post. We sell anything. We find anything. Nothing impossible.*

Suddenly I felt as if I were having a vision. I was back with Gerry at the hamburger restaurant. I could see her waving the newspaper at me and laughing. I could hear myself saying, "I'm not that desperate yet!"

Well, maybe I was that desperate now. I moved as if I

were hypnotized. I tore a sheet from the notepad in my purse and printed on it with my mangled pencil stub: *Wanted: Mature male student to escort cute girl to fun party.* Then I scribbled in my first name and telephone number and pinned it onto the board before I had time to think.

Chapter Twelve

IT ACTUALLY took me until Monday morning to realize just what I had done. I couldn't believe that I
would do a thing like that! My phone number was now
on the college bulletin board. Anyone might call this
house. What if a mature college guy did call, and when
he found out that I was the girl, he got mad, or worse
still, he laughed? What if the college president called
because notices like that weren't allowed? And what if
he called and my father answered?

I didn't have time to go up to the college before
school to take the note down, and I worried about it
all day. Gerry passed me in the hall at lunchtime.

"You look like someone who's just discovered ring
around the collar," she said, not unkindly. "Are you
worrying that your wonderful guy won't show up for
the dance, maybe?" She said it as a tease, with a twin-
kle in her eye. I knew, at the back of my mind somewhere, that she was taking the first step toward
making up, but she was also touching a very raw
nerve. Why did she have to be such a smart mouth all
the time?

"I'm worrying about the math test, if you want to know," I said coldly. "The formal is all arranged, thank you. I'm just waiting to watch your look of envy when I walk in." Then I stalked away.

After that I felt even more terrible. I missed Gerry and I really wanted to be friends with her. It was just that I felt like I was being stretched to the point where I was about to snap, and Gerry was threatening to do the snapping.

I did terribly on the math test. I tried to concentrate but those rows of figures swam up and down in front of my eyes. I think I even added two and two and made them five a few times.

The moment school was out I rushed out the front door and didn't really stop until I was standing in front of the bulletin board outside the Student Center. I looked for my notice. But it was gone. My stomach did a terrible lurch. Someone had taken it down! At this very moment he might be phoning my house and talking to my mother!

Will you calm down, I said to myself, trying to use reason. If someone took down the notice, they will just have thrown it into the nearest trash basket. Why would they want to do anything else with it? The whole problem has been solved for you. The notice has gone, and you can stop worrying.

I felt relieved as I walked home. I didn't know what came over me the night before. I was not the type of girl who could pick up strange men. I never would be that type of girl. Plain Julie Klein, that was me—no sense of adventure at all. For a moment I did just wonder what it would have been like if anyone had answered my ad. Maybe he would have thought I looked mature. Maybe he wouldn't even care that I was a high school student. Maybe...

But it was no use thinking about it. The ad was gone. I was safe and I still had no partner for the Freshman Formal. Everything I did at school reminded me of it. Every art class I was working on those dumb posters. Ironically, they were the one thing that was going well in my life. I was getting more confident in splodging on all those bright colors, and Mrs. Wright was impressed.

"Why, Julie, that's beautiful," she said. "I'd really like to give you something a little more ambitious to do—maybe a big mural if you have time."

I was glad of the praise but annoyed that it only came from a teacher. I wished Gary had stopped by and said, "Hey Julie, great-looking painting. Why don't you help me with mine sometime?" Then I remembered that Gary thought that I turned my nose up at little high school kids. Besides, he couldn't afford to take me to expensive restaurants or home in taxis.

Even Phillip Kaufman didn't talk to me much anymore. Except about work. I don't think he had gotten over being snubbed the night of the concert. I felt guilty about that too. It was as if I were carrying a heavy load of guilt no matter what I did. I felt like yelling, "Let's go back to the way it was a few weeks ago, back when I had Gerry as a best friend and I had never heard about the dumb Freshman Formal." Some days I would even have welcomed a good conversation with Phillip...which shows how desperate I was getting.

One day during lunch I wandered into the art room to put the finishing touches to my latest poster, and he was there. He jumped guiltily as I entered.

"Oh hi," I said. "I didn't think anyone would be here. I came to add a bit more red to that cape."

"It's over there on the counter," he said, gathering up his papers.

"Hey, don't leave on my account," I said. "I won't disturb you."

"No, I'd better get some lunch anyway," he said. He put his papers into a pile and started shoveling pencils into a pouch. Then he left. Before he went I got a good look at the top paper. It was the most beautiful drawing of a knight on a horse doing battle with a dragon. Much better than I could have done. Yet all his work in class was so ordinary, drawn well but without any soul. This drawing was so alive it glowed. Maybe one day I'd have the courage to ask him about it—after I had sorted out the formal.

Right after lunch I ran into Caroline. I had been trying to find excuses not to join them at lunch because I just didn't enjoy it anymore. They cut everybody down all the time while seeming totally sweet.

"Hey Julie, wait up," Caroline called down the hall to me. "Where've you been all day?"

"I have to work on this art project for the formal," I said. "I don't have much time for lunch these days."

"Oh, too bad," she said. "But don't waste too much time on it. After all, who is going to be looking up at the walls? We'll all be busy doing much more important things. Will you lend me Danny for just one dance? I'd love to see Russ's face..."

"I'll have to think about it," I said. "I don't even know if Danny can come. It's his finals week. I may invite another guy."

"Another guy—what would Danny say?"

"Oh, just a friend," I said. "Danny won't mind."

"No, I suppose not. He's mature about these things," Caroline said. "Russ would blow his top if I wanted to go somewhere with another guy. But do try to persuade Danny to come. I am just dying to meet him!"

Little does she know, I thought gloomily as we walked on together down the hall. And when she does know, she will drop me like a ton of bricks.

"So what are you wearing to the formal, Julie?" Caroline asked.

"I...don't know yet," I said. "I can't make up my mind." I was about to say that I'd probably find something at the Gladrags Boutique in the mall, or maybe at Macy's. Before I could say any of this, Caroline went on talking, as usual. She asked a question but didn't really want an answer. She was already on the next subject by the time you opened your mouth.

"I don't know what some of the dresses will look like this year," she said, chuckling to herself. "Do you know that some girls are actually buying their dresses in that tatty little Gladrags Boutique in the mall. I mean, what poor taste! I wouldn't use anything they had as a dishrag. I bet you go into the city for all your shopping, don't you? Maybe we could go in together one day?"

"Maybe," I said, feeling torn between the delight that Caroline actually considered me a person she'd like to go shopping with and the bad taste in my mouth that she had put down the store where half the school shopped, including me!

Is this what I'm aiming for? I asked myself on the way home. To be friends with someone who puts down everyone else? The trouble was that Caroline was fun. I laughed a lot when I was around her. I got a lot of admiring glances when I was around Russ. It didn't really matter whether I liked them or not, because I knew, one hundred percent, that if I were in with them, I'd be accepted by the whole school. Only, of course, now I wouldn't be in with them. I'd have to tell Caroline that I wouldn't be going shopping, because I didn't need a dress at all.

I drifted through the next couple of days in a cloud of gloom and had almost put the ad out of my mind— which was why I was totally taken by surprise when I answered the phone on Thursday evening.

"Get that, will you, Julie?" my mother had called from the kitchen. "It will be Aunt Elaine and I'm up to my elbows in flour."

I picked up the phone. "Hi!" I said cheerfully.

"Oh, hello . . ." a voice said cautiously on the other end. "Am I speaking to the young lady about the party?"

"Excuse me?" I asked, thrown off balance by the deep male voice. For a moment I couldn't think of what he was talking about.

"You, er, did put the ad on the college bulletin board, didn't you?" he asked hesitantly. "I did call the right number?"

"Oh, yes," I said. I could hardly make my lips move. I was only glad he couldn't see me, standing there in my

old warm-up suit with a half-eaten grilled cheese sand-
wich in one hand and my face flaming red.

"I saw your ad on the bulletin board," he went on.

Pause.

"That's right."

Another pause.

"Are you a student at the college?"

"Not exactly. Just part-time." (The lie just slipped out
before I could stop it.) "Are you?"

"Oh, yes. I'm planning to transfer to Columbia next
fall."

That sounded good. After all, Columbia was almost
as good as Yale. I hated to be a snob! Suddenly I only
wanted Ivy League! Sometimes I surprised myself.

Another long pause. I heard him clearing his throat.
"I wondered if...that is, I thought we might perhaps
...before the party, you know–meet somewhere. Get
to know each other. I might not be the kind of person
you had in mind. Does that sound like a good idea?"

"Oh–sure," I stammered. "That's a good idea."

"Where do you suggest we meet?" he asked. "I'm
available anytime. How about this weekend?"

"That's fine."

"Saturday afternoon maybe?"

"Fine."

"How about the railway station? I always think railway stations are good impersonal places to meet."

"The station would be fine."

"Shall we say under the clock? At three o'clock?"

"Fine."

"That's settled, then. I really look forward to meeting
you, er, Miss..."

88

"Julie."

"Ah, Julie. I'm Ronald. Until Saturday then, Julie."

"Until Sat—hey, wait a minute. How will I recognize you?"

"Oh, silly me. Good question. How about we both wear a flower? Under the clock and wearing a flower. OK?"

"OK."

"That's great, Julie. Goodbye now."

"Goodbye, Ronald."

I stood there in the hall for a long time after he had hung up. I wasn't quite sure whether to laugh or cry. I was meeting someone called Ronald, wearing a flower, under the clock at the railway station. It was too much like something out of a bad spy movie. Maybe I should have given him a password, I thought, giggling. It hadn't exactly been a romantic conversation; still, you could never tell over the phone. He might be tall, dark and shy. I hadn't sounded too great either. All I could remember saying was "fine" about two hundred times. And he was a college student, about to transfer to Columbia.

The more I thought about it, the better it seemed. All Saturday morning I wished that Gerry would call and ask me to do something with her in the afternoon so that I could tell her I had a date with a college student instead. I spent a long time getting ready. Every outfit I had seemed too juvenile and made me look about twelve years old. I put on more makeup than ever before and ended up looking like a clown. Finally I settled on the outfit my mother had bought me last year. I didn't particularly like it. The shade of blue was a little too bright for my coloring. I hadn't wanted to wear it and complained that it made me look like the world's youngest secretary. But somehow today the straight blue skirt and the tailored striped blouse created the look I wanted, or as close to the look I wanted without buying a new outfit. At least it was one stage better than my usual jeans and a sweatshirt. I fought with my hair to make it stay back, and by the time I had finished I thought that I could pass for a college freshman.

Since my father wasn't the world's greatest gardener, no flowers grew in our front yard, so I broke a spray of almond blossom off our neighbor's tree and tucked that into my blue jacket. Then I set out to meet my destiny!

It was a beautiful day. The sky was that clear glass-blue you only get between spring showers. The air smelled fresh and spring-cleaned, and the birds were singing crazily to each other. It was almost a Walt Disney-movie kind of day. I almost felt I was expected to break into a song-and-dance routine with a few blue-birds flying around me and a couple of rabbits hopping behind. Surely the weather was a good omen that today was finally going to be *my* day, that everything was finally going to go right.

I pictured the scene at the station again and again in my mind. By this time I had given Ronald a very distinct personality—he was studious, like Danny, only not quite as cute. He had spent so much time on his studies that he hadn't had too much practice with dates. He probably didn't even realize how good-looking he was when he took off those glasses. He would be standing there, half hidden by a pillar as I came toward him. He would see me, notice the flower, and his eyes would light up. When he smiled, his eyes would crinkle at the sides, and his whole face would sort of glow, so that you could tell at once he was a nice person with a great sense of humor.

"How about meeting like this?" he would say. "Doesn't it remind you of a bad spy story? I should have thought of somewhere more original, but I'm very bad on the phone. I sort of clam up. Do you know the feeling?"

Then we'd walk together through the park, and we'd discover that we liked all the same things and that he was an only child, too. We'd go to the ice cream parlor and laugh when we found out that we both liked chocolate-chocolate chip, chocolate-dipped on a sugar cone, and that we had both sworn to eat a whole Matterhorn one day. When I finally told him about the Freshman Formal, he would say that he didn't go in for dances much, but he could see how important it was for me...

The blaring of a taxicab horn brought me down to earth and made me realize that I had been daydreaming and almost crossed against a red light. Coming down to reality with a sharp jolt like that scared the sweet daydream away. When I tried to recreate it, it wouldn't come back. I couldn't even picture Ronald's face clearly anymore. As I crossed the bridge toward the station, I realized that I was very, very nervous. The "what-ifs" started flying again, worse than ever before: What if he takes one look at me and says, "But

you're only a little kid. Is this some sort of joke?" And
then he laughs. What if I can't think of anything to say
and I blush, and he thinks I'm stupid and he suddenly
remembers that he has a class assignment to finish?

I walked round the outside of the station four times
before I dared go in. I just can't do this, I kept telling
myself. I can't go up to a strange guy... The what-ifs
became one stage more terrible. What if he's not a student at all, but a crazy guy who uses chances like this
to lure young girls away, and he suggests driving up
into the hills? I can't handle this, I thought, as my
stomach did double somersaults. I'm not mature. I
don't belong with a college guy. That was just a stupid
dream.

I actually turned and started walking away from the
station again.

But you did get on so well with Danny, I argued
back to myself. And what if you're throwing away the
one chance of your life? What if this is really the guy
you have been waiting for? What if you are the girl he
has been waiting for?

I turned back toward the station. What have you got
to lose? I asked myself. It's the middle of the afternoon. What can happen? If you don't like the look of
him you don't have to go anywhere with him.

I walked up the station steps, one at a time. The in-
terior glowed with a gloomy green light like an aquarium. Noises echoed loudly from the marble floor to the
high ceiling—the screech of a whistle, the clatter of
running feet, the slamming of train doors and all the
time the murmur of voices. I found myself walking on
tiptoe, creeping around the edge, past the bookstand

and the ladies' room and the candy kiosk. Why did the clock have to be right on the other side of the building? A couple of people looked at me and I remembered how dumb I must look with the stupid flower pinned to my jacket.

At first I couldn't see anyone under the clock, except a lady with two little kids. Then I noticed the flower. It was a big daffodil, bright yellow. Nobody could miss it. He was staring out across the lobby, his eyes on the front door, expecting me to come straight across from that direction. Thank heavens he was, or he would have seen me before I had a chance to rip off my almond blossom and stuff it into my pocket. I stood behind a pillar, panting as if I had just run a marathon, feeling the cold of the marble against my back. Then I started to run, feet clattering across that echoing floor, pushing people out of my way until I was outside with the warm spring sun shining down on me and birds singing and life going on just as it always had before.

Why hadn't I realized that this might happen? Suppose I had been a second later and he had seen me? I squirmed with embarrassment as I crossed the street, safely far away from that station. He hadn't looked like a bad person; in fact the face I had seen peering out across the lobby had seemed kind and friendly. But it was an old face —I mean, really old. Thirty, maybe. His hair was already starting to thin on top. His clothes were the sort of clothes men wear to relax in—a tweed jacket and beige cords and a tie and even a patterned sweater peeping out underneath! Until that moment I hadn't realized that mature could mean different things to different people.

Chapter Thirteen

I DONT THINK I stopped running until I got home.

"Why, Julie, what's the matter?" my mother asked, trying to grab me as I burst in through the front door.

"If the phone rings, don't answer it," I panted. "Or say I'm not here or moved away or something."

"But what happened?" my mother called after me. I was already halfway up the stairs.

"Nothing. I don't want to talk about it, OK?" I yelled. Then I shut my bedroom door behind me and leaned against it. How could I possibly tell my mother what had happened? How could I ever explain what made me do such a dumb thing and how scared I was when I saw him standing there? I could picture him again now, every detail of his face, the way his hair was combed forward, his terrible clothes and the daffodil stuck through a buttonhole. Then I suddenly realized something—he was still waiting there, hoping that I would be somebody else, too.

I remembered another detail about him—how his eyes were riveted on the main entrance, waiting for me to come. How long would he continue to stand there waiting until he decided that I wasn't coming, ever?

I walked slowly across the room and picked up my old rag doll from my pillow. My grandmother had made her for me just before she died, when I was about three years old. I couldn't really remember much of my grandmother, except that her house had a warm, comfortable, secure feeling about it, and she sat me on her knee while we looked at family photos together. "And there's your Mommie when she was just a little girl, no bigger than you." I would stare unbelieving at the faded black and white picture of a girl who looked a bit like me, wearing a frilly dress and holding a big doll in one hand. "Where's her dolly now, grandma?" I asked. "I wish I had one like that."

I hugged my doll to me, remembering how happy I had been when my grandma made me one. Now I noticed that the doll's neck was coming unstitched and stuffing was oozing out on one side. Why couldn't things stay the way they were when I was little? Suddenly life had become complicated. I couldn't handle it anymore, and who could I tell? If I went downstairs and told my mother, she probably wouldn't understand.

"That was a stupid thing to do, Julie, but you could just have gone up to the man and confessed that you had made a mistake," she would say.

I had escaped without making a fool of myself. I could go back to being an immature high school student, without a date and without a hope of a date ... except for one thing. I had a bad taste in my mouth about leaving Ronald standing there. For the first time, I had been in a position of real power over somebody else and I had let him down. I could imagine all too clearly how it would have felt if *I* had been the person standing there, waiting and hoping. It didn't matter how old Ronald was—he was obviously a shy person like me. I remembered how he had sounded on the phone—not at all sure of himself. Perhaps this would be the final blow for him, and he would decide never to meet girls again and go live in a monastery, or worse, all because of me!

I had no way of making it right. My panic had gone and I realized that he wouldn't call again. He would be like me and not have the nerve to be rejected twice. I had no way of getting in touch with him to tell him I was sorry. Unless...a sudden thought crossed my mind. I could put up another notice on the college bulletin board!

I'm not going near that place again, I told myself firmly. But you owe it to Ronald, I argued back. Nothing can happen if you sneak in and put up a notice. Nobody will ever be able to trace it to you, and Ronald will feel happier.

I took a long time to compose it, filling my wastebasket with crumpled balls of my best unicorn notepaper. Finally I wrote: *Ronald. Sorry about Saturday. Things have changed, and I can't make the party anymore. Julie.*

I read it through about three hundred times, to make sure that it wouldn't give him any wrong ideas about getting together again. Then I decided to take it up to the college right away.

"Are you going out again?" my mother called. "I wish you'd tell me what's going on."

"Nothing's going on," I said. "I need some exercise, and I'm going out for a walk."

"But you seemed so upset earlier," she said. "Are you in some sort of trouble? You can talk to me, you know. I'm your mother. I want to help."

I could see from her face that she was imagining the worst, and it sort of amused me that she believed I had had the time to get into any bad trouble. The only boys I had ever dated had been Eagle Scouts and sang in church choirs. Perhaps she thought I was taking drugs at school! My mother led a sheltered life but was carried away by what she read in the newspaper.

I smiled. "Look, Mom, I just had a little mix-up with a friend this afternoon, but it's not important. I'm not in any trouble. I'm just going out for a walk, and I'll be back soon, OK?"

"OK, Julie," she said, but I don't think she quite believed me.

The hall with the bulletin board was deserted. I pinned the note up next to an ad for a 1963 VW Beetle and walked back home again.

I'm glad Gerry and I aren't speaking to each other, I thought. At least nobody in the whole world knows how dumb I have been.

I hardly spoke all through dinner. I wanted to settle down to watch TV. Things are really bad when TV reruns are the highlight of life, I thought, but at least I was relaxed again, back into my comfortable, boring routine.

I didn't even hear the phone ring.

"Julie, there's a call for you!" my father yelled.

"The phone? For me?" I asked. I could feel the blood draining out of my face. "Who is it?" I asked suspiciously.

"He didn't say."

"You mean it's a boy?"

"Either that or a girl with a very deep voice," my father said, grinning at his own joke. I stood there as if I had been turned to stone.

"Ask him if his name's Ronald," I said.

My father went back to the phone. "He says his name is not Ronald," he called. "For heaven's sake come and take this thing. It's for you."

I took the phone as if it were a live snake. I couldn't think of any boy in the world who would be phoning me.

"Hello?" My voice definitely quivered as I spoke.

"Well, hi there," came the voice on the other end, still unidentifiable. "Are you the girl who likes to party?"

"Who likes to what?" I stammered. "I think you must have the wrong number."

"Aren't you the girl who put up the notice?" He sounded disappointed. "The one who likes a fun time?"

"Oh that," I said. "Yes, I did put it up, but it was all a mistake. I mean, a joke, sort of."

"Oh...you mean you don't like a fun time after all, and you're not going to the terrific party? Or do you already have a date?"

His voice was full of confidence. I could almost hear him laughing and teasing me on the other end of the line. I was feeling more and more confused. "No–I mean yes."

"No, you don't have a date, or yes, you do?" he asked.

"No, I don't," I said. "But I'm not sure–"

"Hey, listen, that's great," he interrupted. "I'm new in town. I transferred here this semester, and I haven't met many fun girls yet. How about you and me going out tonight? Then you can tell me all about your party and see if you'd want to take me along."

I gulped. "Tonight?"

"Unless you're *busy*." He made the word busy have a million undertones.

"No, I'm—"

"Great. Why don't I come around to your house to pick you up in an hour. Since we're both free, we might as well get together now. Do you like dancing? I've found this great club about five miles out on the highway. The Last Resort—do you know it?"

"No, I don't, but look, I—"

"Oh, the music is really great. Not real heavy rock. The sort of music you can really dance to, including slow numbers...I know you'd like it."

I stood there not saying anything. This can't be happening to me, I kept thinking. I could tell from his voice, from his easy laugh, that he was not going to be another Ronald. In fact he sounded a lot like Danny. Almost too good to be true.

"Are you still there?" he asked. "Or have I bored you to sleep? I can tell you that my former girlfriends didn't find me boring."

"I'm here," I said. "I was just trying to make up my mind about this evening. It's just that...I've gotten suspicious about blind dates. Even though I put up the sign, I'm really shy."

"Shy. Sure. I understand. Had some bad experiences too?" he asked. "Well, I can assure you that with me you'll be fine. My name's Steve, by the way. You're Julie, right?"

"Yes, that's right. I'm Julie."

"Nice name. And you have a nice voice, too. I bet you have green eyes."

"Well, sort of bluish green. How did you know?"

"I can always tell. Green eyes are my favorite. So what do you say, Julie—can I come around and pick you up so we can have a good time?"

"Look, Steve. Can I ask you a question?"

"What do you want to know about me? I'm studying engineering, and I'm not married, and I don't live with my aged mother, and I like dogs and children and pepperoni pizza and funny movies. I'm six feet one and I weigh a hundred and seventy five, and I used to go out for track in high school, and I have black hair and brown eyes and no disfiguring marks on my face. Does that answer your question?"

"Perfectly," I said, starting to laugh in disbelief that this could be happening at all, let alone to me of all people.

"And I'll make you another guarantee," he said. "If you take one look at my face and scream, you don't have to go through with the date. OK?"

"OK," I said.

"Terrific. Give me your address, and I'll see you soon."

As I put down the phone, I caught sight of my face in the mirror that hangs in our hall. I looked flushed and excited. My eyes were shining.

Now what have you done? I asked myself.

Chapter Fourteen

I ABSOLUTELY flew up the stairs. I had to get ready for the most important date in my life.

"Julie?" my mother called as I reached the top step.

"Not now, Mom." I called down to her.

"What's happening, Julie? Who was that on the phone?"

"It was a friend, Mom, and he's coming to pick me up, and I don't want him to see me like this."

"You mean a *boy*, Julie? You are going out with a *boy?*"

"That's right. Now can I go get dressed?"

"Who is this boy?" my mother asked suspiciously. She came up the stairs after me. I turned and went ahead of her into my room, rummaging through my drawers for the right sort of clothes to wear dancing with a six-foot-one, black-haired guy.

"You don't know him," I said. "He's a friend of a friend."

"Someone from your school?"

"Not exactly."

"Where? Where did you meet him?"

"It's a long story. But trust me. This is a good thing

for me. I'm only going out with him—I don't want to marry him or anything."

"How long have you known him, Julie?"

I pulled a red top of Gerry's out of the drawer. It had glitter over one shoulder, and I didn't think I would ever dare wear it. But tonight it would go with those tight red pants. "Long enough," I answered. "I've known him a while." I didn't like to tell lies, and "a while" can mean anything from ten seconds upwards.

"Why haven't you told us about him before? You could have brought him to meet us before he took you on a date."

"Oh, Mom, this isn't the dark ages, you know. Parents aren't supposed to give dates the once-over anymore. And this isn't really a date. There is absolutely nothing to worry about. He's a nice guy and I'll be home early. OK?"

I started to wriggle into the red pants.

"Well, I may be old-fashioned," my mother said, "but I want to know what sort of boy is taking my daughter out for an evening. You haven't had much experience with boys yet, and I worry about you. And don't you think those red pants are a bit too bright and a bit too tight?"

"They're the fashion, Mom. Like you said, you are old-fashioned," I said, holding my breath while I zipped them up. "Don't worry so much."

"As your mother, I have the right to worry, but I suppose you're right," she said. She turned toward the door. "I thought we had a good relationship, Julie," she added. "But the past few weeks you've changed. I hope it's only a phase you're going through."

I could hear the hurt in her voice. It made me feel terrible, but I just couldn't risk spoiling this evening. Maybe I would be able to have a good time *and* get a date for the formal. I knew without a doubt that she would not let me go out with a college guy I had never even met.

"I'm a big girl now, Mom," I said to her as she walked out of my room. "You've got to trust me and let me live my own life."

She turned back, and this time I could see the hurt in her face. "I do trust you," she said, "but I want to save you from doing anything you'd regret later. We can't help being concerned about you. After all, you are our only child. You're all we've got."

"Oh, Mom," I said shaking my head in disbelief. "It's just a friendly evening with a guy, OK? I'm not serious or anything. Just like the day I spent with Danny. Now you didn't worry about that, did you?"

"He's your cousin," my mother said firmly. "I'd have worried if he'd been a stranger. But I suppose you wouldn't do anything foolish. Just make sure you are back before midnight, that's all. Your father and I don't want to stay up all night pacing the floor and biting our fingernails."

Then she gave me a kiss and went downstairs. I hurriedly pulled on the red glitter top, caught my hair back on one side with a red comb and gave myself big dark eyes and red lips.

"Steve." I whispered his name as I thought about the voice on the phone. It had a nice sound to it. "Steve and Julie. Julie and Steve. Oh, hi there, Caroline. This is Steve. Did I introduce you to Steve yet, Gerry?" And Gerry would drag me aside at the first opportunity. "What a gorgeous hunk," she would say. "Where did you find him?"

I would smile calmly. "You just have to know where to look. Did I ever tell you about the fantastic night we had at the Last Resort—you know, that club out on the highway? Steve took me into his arms and kissed me. Oh, but don't let me go on so."

The doorbell woke me instantly from the magic of that kiss. I flew down the stairs before either of my parents could reach the front door first. I glanced at myself nervously in the hall mirror. Was my makeup too bright? Was that glitter top too sexy? Would my hair stay obediently back? Did I look too young?

The doorbell rang again. "I've got it," I called, and opened the front door.

"Hi," said a warm, deep voice, and I found myself looking up into the face I had dreamed about.

Chapter Fifteen

FOR A MOMENT I wondered if I had finally gone too far with my fantasizing and was seeing someone who didn't really exist. But then he reached out and touched my arm, making me only too painfully aware of his existence.

"Hi," he said again, smiling as if he were used to the effect he caused on poor, unsuspecting girls who were meeting him for the first time. "You are Julie, aren't you? I'm Steve."

"Hi," I managed to say, wittily, before I turned around to make sure my mother had not crept out of the living room to overhear this conversation. I knew there was no way she would let me leave the house with a guy I had just met for the first time, even if that guy did look like my knight in shining armor.

"You look great," he said, eyeing me up from my toes to my hair as if I were a mannequin in a department store. "You ready to roll?"

Just as he said this, I heard the living room door open behind me with a great burst of laughter from the TV set.

"Was that the doorbell, Julie?" my mother's voice called. "Dad said he thought he heard—"

"Yes, Mom," I called back. "I'm just leaving. See you later. Bye." And I closed the door firmly behind me before hurrying ahead of Steve down to the car. Tonight nothing was going to stop me, not even my overprotective parents!

Even the car was perfect—a white English sports car with a top that folded down in good weather.

"In a big hurry to escape?" Steve asked as he opened the door for me. He gave me a wink that made me melt right down to my toes.

If only Gerry would come out of her house right at this minute, I thought. It would be worth everything in my whole life to have her see me drive off like this. This would show her who had learned to survive in the real world!

Steve sprang in lightly and we roared away down the empty street. Much as I was enjoying it, I did realize that we were going way over the speed limit. I glanced around nervously again. Steve reached out and touched my hand. "Hey, relax," he said. "I am an expert at knowing which stretch of the highway the cops actually patrol. And it's never this bit. I am always very careful. I can't afford to get a ticket or they'll raise my insurance rates again." And while he talked, he flashed a quick smile in my direction, his eyes challenging mine.

He kept up a constant stream of talk, telling me about the problems and expense of his car engine, his weird landlady, jobs he had had and lost, jobs he hoped to get one day and even his dog when he was a little boy. I only had to grunt every now and then to show I was still listening, and everything he said seemed exciting and funny. I thought about Gerry's date, who had only talked about cars. I thought about Danny and his bugs, and I could hardly believe my luck. Here was someone who was great-looking and funny and not at all boring. He even seemed to enjoy being with me.

I could see the flashing neon sign from way off, just as I had imagined. The club itself looked elegant and expensive, and the cars in the parking lot told you straight away that kids didn't go there. The music was throbbing, but less wild than I had imagined. When we went inside it wasn't deafening, which was another good thing. The band consisted of a keyboard player, a drummer and a man who played the flute and the saxophone, depending on the song. Caroline and Russ would probably have laughed at them and called them hopelessly old-fashioned, but tonight their music seemed just right.

The room was not very large, and small tables were crowded around the walls, each lit by a candle. The air was full of smoke, which swirled magically through the spotlight on the band. It was almost as I had pictured it. The waitress came over, and Steve ordered a bottle of wine. I waited for him to order a coke for me, but he didn't.

"I thought you said you were only twenty," I whispered as the waitress walked away. "You're under the drinking age, too."

He laughed. "I guess I just look older," he said. "No one ever asks me to show my ID."

"But I can't drink wine," I said.

He went on laughing. "Sure you can. No one's going

to question your age either. We look like an old, so-phisticated couple. Here, let me pour you a glass."

I watched, wondering what to do next. Gerry was al-ways drinking wine. I knew her parents even let her at home, and she didn't show any signs of turning into an alcoholic. My parents had never let me drink, except for one glass of champagne at a wedding last year. That hadn't tasted at all bad. Steve picked up my glass and put it into my hand. "Cheers," he said, clinking my glass to his. I took a sip. It was cold and slipped down easily.

He sat across the table from me, the candlelight making his eyes sparkle. I actually pinched myself a couple of times to make sure I wasn't dreaming.

"What are you staring at?" he asked once. "Is some-thing wrong?"

"Oh no," I said. "It's just that you remind me so much—"

"Don't tell me—of your last boyfriend," he quipped. "That's what all the girls say. I must have a universal face."

"No. Actually," I said, "you remind me of a guy in an old picture. A knight fighting a dragon."

Steve threw back his head and laughed. "That really is a new one," he said. "I don't think that would have been me in one of my past lives. I have always been much too sensible to fight dragons. I would have let some other guy do the fighting, and while he was busy I would have untied the princess and sneaked off with her."

"Oh."

"Well, don't take it so seriously," he said, smiling. "I

guess I don't go in for dragons and stuff too much. I outgrew fantasy years ago. I find real life is much more exciting, don't you?"

"I hope so," I said cautiously.

"Here," he said, touching my hand. "Drink up. I'll fill your glass for you again."

We talked for a while, then we danced and he held me just as close as I had imagined he would. Then we talked some more and danced some more. I felt myself feeling more at ease with him. He laughed at the little jokes I made, all the time teasing me with his eyes. I felt as if I were floating through a wonderful dream. Tonight, I kept telling myself, I am going to have my first real kiss. And it's going to be just as I always hoped...

Around eleven a group of noisy kids came in, and immediately the band switched to blaring music, so loud that the candle flames seemed to shake on the tables.

"This really isn't my kind of music," Steve yelled above the noise. "Let's leave now, OK?"

We walked out into the crisp night air. The full moon was floating in the sky, just as if I had ordered it. Now he was going to take me in his arms and kiss me...

"It's freezing out here," he said, shivering. "Jump in and let's get going."

Balloon number one popped. Maybe I had been reading too much into the way he felt about me, I thought, sitting there feeling disappointed. I could still feel his arms around me as we danced, my cheek against his shoulder, his hand holding mine as we walked back to the table. Surely I couldn't have been wrong. And the way his eyes seemed to bore right into mine. Didn't a guy only look at a girl like that when he wanted to kiss her?

"Are you tired?" he asked suddenly. "You're awfully quiet."

"No, I'm not tired," I said. "Although I guess we'd better be heading towards my house pretty soon. I have to be in before midnight."

"Or you turn into a pumpkin?" he asked, flashing me a smile.

"No, the wicked witch will be waiting to turn me into something much worse," I said, smiling back.

"What could be worse than a pumpkin?" he asked. "Just think of lying there, big and fat, out in the cold field until somebody starts carving faces into you and then shreds you up for a pie. Come to think of it, pumpkin pie is one of the things I hate most in life."

"Me too," I said. "I hate gooey texture."

"See," he said, "what a lot of things we have in common?"

The warm feeling was creeping back up from my toes again. He hadn't not wanted to kiss me. It really had been too cold out there. But here in the car would be ideal...

He brought the car to a halt beside a tall old house on the edge of town.

"Where are we?" I asked. I peered out and tried to focus on hundreds of stone steps, going up and up, and window after window of blazing lights. Even though my head felt a bit fuzzy, I knew that this was no place I had seen before. If he was planning to park and get to the kissing, this seemed an odd place to do it, so public and brightly lit.

"Oh, this is where I live," he said. "I need to pick up some gloves. My hands are freezing on this steering wheel. You want to come up for a minute?"

Chapter Sixteen

WE SEEMED to be climbing a million stairs. Bursts of music or a shriek of laughter came from behind doors we passed. My legs were beginning to feel like jelly, and still the stairs went on. When I stumbled against the stair rail, Steve put his arm around my waist to steady me. I was glad he did because everything swung around and around. "Only one more flight," he said, and kept his arm there. "I guess I have gotten so used to this mountaineering every day that I don't realize what five flights seem like to other people."

"If I'd known you lived at the top of the World Trade Center, I would have stayed in the car," I said. For some reason I was finding it hard to make the words come out the way I wanted them.

"You wouldn't have let me go all this way on my own, would you?" Steve whispered in my ear.

At last we were at the top of the building. There was a skylight in the ceiling above our heads. I stared up at it while Steve fished for his key, but it started swinging around too, so I looked down again hastily. Steve opened the bright yellow door in front of us. "Here we are," he said. "Home, Sweet Home."

The only guys' rooms I had ever seen before were Gerry's brothers'. Those were usually such a horrible mess of clutter that you couldn't find the furniture. I guess I thought all boys' rooms would be like that. But this one was totally different. There was almost no furniture in it. When Steve turned on the light, it threw a pink glow onto some floor pillows and a huge mattress covered with a zebra patterned rug. The coffee table beside it had a neat pile of textbooks stacked beside an expensive looking stereo.

"Sorry about the furniture," Steve said, grinning at me. 'Or rather the lack of it." He took my hand and led me into the room, shutting the door firmly behind us.

"I have expensive taste, unfortunately, so I won't buy anything permanent until I can afford good stuff. And since I don't have a job, and my car keeps eating every penny of my savings, I guess I'm going to be living on the floor for a few more years."

"That's fine with me," I said. "I spend most of my time on the floor."

"I knew we'd get on just fine," he said. "Would you like a drink?"

"Oh, I think we'd better just get your gloves and go," I said.

"My what?" he asked, looking amused.

"We came up here for your gloves, remember?"

"Oh yes, my gloves," he said, smiling to himself as if he just remembered a funny story. "But there's really no hurry. We're only five minutes from your house, and pumpkin time is not for another half hour or more. Sit down a minute. Make yourself comfortable. I'm really thirsty after all that smoke at the club. Sure you don't want a glass of 7-Up?"

"Well, if you're going to have one," I said hesitantly. Suddenly my legs had become incredibly heavy, as if they didn't want to support my weight a minute longer. I sank down onto the nearest floor pillow. It was big and soft, and it felt like sinking into one of those fluffy clouds I had tried to paint.

"That's more like it," Steve said, returning with a tray and two glasses. He put the tray on the floor, then joined me on the floor pillow.

"Comfortable?" he asked, slipping an arm behind my neck.

"Mmmm," I said dreamily. The floating feeling had come back again so that it was like being on a raft, swaying gently in an ocean.

"Terrific," he said. "I've really had a great time this evening... I'm glad I finally met someone like you. I began to think I'd have to transfer back home again..."

His lips were close to my ear as he talked. They nuzzled at my ear and my cheek before finally meeting mine.

I suppose this couldn't really count as my first kiss, because a couple of my dates had attempted half-hearted meetings of our lips. I had imagined my first real kiss for years—the sort of kiss you read about in books when you soar to the moon. But in my imagination it had always been a little hesitant and shy, as if the boy and I were both overcome with the wonder of it. This kiss was in no way hesitant. And through that persistent floating feeling came a stronger, scared feeling that first kisses shouldn't be like this. With a great effort I leaped up.

"What's wrong, baby?" Steve murmured.

"We've only just met, that's what's wrong," I said. I struggled to move away from him and sit up.

"Oh come on," he crooned. "We were getting along so well. I told you we were right for each other. Just relax. It's OK. Nobody's going to come in or anything."

"That's not the point," I said.

"What *is* the point?" he asked, propping himself up on his elbow and looking at me with hard, dark eyes. "Don't you like me?"

"Of course I like you," I said. "You're good looking. At first you seemed nice, but I just can't handle all this. I mean I'm not ready..."

"Oh, come on," he said angrily. "Don't pull that little-girl stuff with me."

"I told you, Steve," I said firmly. "I'm just not ready for this sort of relationship yet."

"What relationship?" he asked. "I wasn't about to offer you a relationship. Just tonight...you and me and a good time. Isn't that what you wanted?"

"No!" I said, feeling myself hot with embarrassment. "I mean, yes, a good time. But not like this..."

"So what sort of good time did you expect?" he snapped. "I mean you put an ad on the college board for all the world to see, you go to a club with a guy you don't even know, you come up to his room when he invites you, and then you start acting like a little schoolgirl!"

"Well, that's what I am!" I said, choking back a sob that was creeping up into my throat. "I *am* a little schoolgirl. I'm only fifteen, and I never wanted something like this."

Steve looked at me as if he didn't believe me. "You're kidding," he said, his mouth half twitching into a laugh. "You're trying to tell me you're only in high school?"

I nodded my head. I couldn't make myself speak anymore.

"Oh no," Steve said, and he sunk his head into his hands. "I had no idea. I thought you were a girl from the college. You're just a little kid. What on earth did you think you were doing, putting an ad like that on the college board? Was it a dare or something?"

"No," I said, gulping the sob back again. "I really thought I'd meet a college guy that way. I wanted to impress the other kids at school and take a college guy to our formal. It sounds silly now, doesn't it?"

Steve was still looking at me and shaking his head, as if he didn't believe what he saw. "You really need your head examined," he said at last. "Do you realize what sort of trouble you could have gotten yourself into?"

"I do now," I said. "I guess I never thought about it."

"Boy, you really must be naive," he said.

"I guess I am," I said. "I wanted to prove that I was mature. I couldn't get the boy in my class I like to notice me, and some kids saw me with my older cousin and they were impressed. So I thought that maybe I was the sort of girl who belonged with older guys." Tears had started to run down my cheeks. I brushed them away. "Dumb, huh?" I said. "I guess I just proved that I'm totally immature and not ready to date anybody yet."

"Hey," he said, reaching over and brushing the tear from my cheek. "It's not as bad as that. You did something dumb, and you've learned a lesson. That's all part of growing up. Of course, you're lucky. If I hadn't been such a terrific person..." He suddenly shot me that wonderful, twisted, wicked smile. "Here, come on," he said, reaching down and pulling me to my feet. "I'll drive you home."

All the way home I shivered. Steve turned the car heating up to high, and I still kept shivering. I could actually hear my teeth chattering. We didn't talk at all. I had a horrible feeling that I had to throw up, and I kept my lips tightly jammed together.

At last we pulled up outside my house. The warm, familiar golden light was streaming out through the glass in the front door. The light in the living room showed that my parents had waited up for me. My mother really cared about me and had been so right about this evening. Lately I'd made her feel that she didn't matter to me anymore. From now on I was going to let her know that she mattered a lot.

As soon as the car came to a complete halt, I put my hand on the door handle. "I'm sorry, Steve," I said. "I really made a fool of myself."

"Being out was better than staying home watching TV," he said, smiling at me. "No, seriously. I had a nice time with you, Julie. I don't know why you have trouble getting boys to notice you at school. Unless you don't find the kind of guy you seem to need."

"I don't know either," I said, opening the door. "But it's a fact. I wish I could get whoever I want, but I guess that's being immature."

I climbed out into the crisp cold air. "Thanks," I said. "I wish I were older."

"Hey Julie," he called, climbing out of the car after me. "I'll come to your dance with you, if that would make your life better. It's no sweat for me—really. I have a sister almost your age. I understand."

"Really?" I asked incredulously. The picture flashed across my mind. Steve looking so mature and handsome, saying witty things to Caroline, making Tracey sigh and even leaving Devon speechless. It was finally being offered to me, just as I had dreamed. They'd never stop talking about Julie Klein if she went to the formal with a gorgeous twenty-year-old.

And then what? I asked myself. Keep on pretending all the rest of my high school career? Keep on acting like someone I'm really not? More hovering between not really fitting in with Caroline's hotshots and no longer belonging with Gerry? I remembered what Steve had said back at the club: "I outgrew fantasy long ago. I find that real life is so much more exciting..."

I looked across at Steve, standing with the streetlight falling like a halo around his head. And I saw him for what he was, just my fantasy. He was a lonely guy who answered an ad. He was nice, but I couldn't bring him to life any more than I could make the dragon slayer step down from the poster on the wall.

I took a deep breath and felt the cold air rush into my lungs. "No thanks," I said. "I've given up pretending to be someone I'm not. I'm really tempted to say yes, but I don't think I could pull it off."

"You see," he beamed. "You're really a mature person after all! Good luck, kid." He bent and gave me a quick peck on my cheek, squeezed my arm and jumped back into his car. Then he revved the engine and roared off into the night.

Chapter Seventeen

THE NEXT MORNING I felt as if a great load had been taken off my shoulders. I didn't have to pretend to be someone I wasn't any longer. I could tell Gerry I was sorry I behaved like such a jerk and wanted to be friends again. I wouldn't have to hang around with Caroline and her crowd, hoping they would finally accept me. This morning I knew, one hundred percent definitely, that I didn't want to become one of them. Most of the time I found their conversation just plain dumb. They were always talking and laughing about other people. Gossip, gossip, gossip—the boys just as bad as the girls. They all acted like big shots, but they were always putting other people down. I knew that *real* big shots never did that. They were comfortable with themselves, and so they didn't need to make other people feel small.

I realized that now I would not be going to the formal and that Caroline and all the others would find out that I wasn't anybody special after all—but suddenly that didn't seem completely earth-shattering. Of course I was disappointed. I had longed to sweep into the hall in a beautiful long dress on the arm of a tall, handsome guy in a white tux. But not if the guy was only taking me because he was doing me a favor. When I finally swept into a dance one day, I wanted the guy to feel as proud of me as I was of him.

So the only part of me that would be going to the formal would be my pictures. I had already completed several bullfight posters, and now Mrs. Wright had asked me to do a big painting of a Mexican town. She had been really pleased with my posters. So I was working in a hurry, trying to cover the big piece of board with the city of Taxco, copied from a postcard.

I was alone in the art room during lunch hour, working on the cathedral towers, which were horribly ornate, when Gerry came in.

"Oh, there you are," she said. "I've been looking everywhere."

"I have to get this finished," I muttered. "It's for the dance."

"That's what I've come to talk to you about," Gerry said. "I'm in charge of the setup and cleanup committee, and I'm trying to get together some people who aren't actually going...I see your name isn't on the ticket list?" she asked after a little pause.

"That's right–I'm not going," I mumbled, still not looking up.

"Well, I'm glad you've finally woken up and stopped pretending," Gerry said.

"What do you mean, 'pretending'?" I snapped, looking up at her for the first time.

"Oh, come on, Julie," she said. "I've been your friend for years. You should be able to trust me. I guessed right away that there wasn't any gorgeous college guy. I know the only college guy you've ever dated was your wimpy cousin!"

I felt anger boiling up inside me. All these years of my being the passive one, following behind Gerry, the popular one, the leader. It was about time she learned a thing or two.

"For your information," I said coldly, "I turned down a gorgeous guy only last night. He offered to take me to the formal, and I turned him down."

"Oh sure," Gerry said, letting a little smile flicker over her lips.

"You don't believe me, do you?"

"No, Julie. I don't believe you."

"Well, it's a pity you weren't outside your house about midnight. Then you would have seen us arrive home, and I could have introduced you to him. He was twenty years old and a super-cute college guy!"

"Julie Klein!" Gerry said angrily. "It's about time you started living in the real world. I know and you know that you are not the type of girl who can go around picking up gorgeous college guys. You don't even have the nerve to speak to guys at school without blushing! You've got to come down to earth and realize you are not some princess who lived years ago, and some guy is not going to come galloping up on a white horse to carry you away. You live in the U.S.A., and perfect guys don't come along that often. And when they do, they won't look at girls like you!"

She grabbed me by the shoulders. "I am not trying to be mean, Julie. I only want to help you. If you spend your life pretending and imagining that a guy from a poster is going to appear, you'll find you're a lonely girl and you'll have nobody!"

"Which just proves how wrong you are, Geraldine Price. There's a lot of things you don't know about me. You think you're the only person in the world who can go around attracting cute guys. Well, I think I can too. And when I find the right one, I'll get him. Believe me, I will."

"You could have the right one now if you weren't so scared of everything," she said. "You're afraid to meet a real guy, which is why you spend all your time dreaming about a guy who is safely a few hundred years away."

"Wrong again," I said coldly. "I had what you would call an exciting date last night. And if you want to know who's scared, I think it's you. You boast that you can get boyfriends. Well, maybe you can—but why don't you keep them? I think you're scared of actually getting involved with anybody, because you don't want to get hurt. That's why you love the theater so much—because it's all pretending."

"That's not true!" she yelled. "I am not scared of anything."

"Then why do you change your boyfriends like library books?" I yelled back. "In fact, I think you are more afraid than I am. At least I'm trying!"

"That's a rotten lie," she screamed. She started shaking me.

"Let go of me!" I shouted.

We were wrestling, right there in the art room.

"I said let go of me!" I yelled even louder. I strug-

gled, then gave her a push. She wasn't expecting such rough treatment from a little mouse like me. She stumbled backwards, put out a hand to save herself and grabbed at my easel. My painting slithered to the ground just behind Gerry, who sat squarely in the middle of it.

For a second we were both frozen with horror. Then she screamed, "My pants!" at the same time I yelled, "My painting!"

Then she seemed to realize what she'd done. She looked down at the brilliant colors, now smudged and decorated liberally with handprints. "Oh no," she said. "Julie, I wrecked your beautiful painting. I'm so sorry."

"It wasn't your fault," I said. "I pushed you backwards."

"But I was trying to interfere with your life again," she said, climbing carefully to her feet. "I've always pushed you around. I guess I deserve to be pushed back. Do you think you can fix it?"

We both stared down at the painting; the tiled rooftops disappeared into an interesting round swirl, and a handprint stuck out of the top of the cathedral.

"It's OK," I said, not knowing whether to laugh or cry. "I couldn't seem to get that cathedral tower right anyway."

"It makes pretty good modern art," Gerry said. "You could call it *Fall of a Matador* or *Death in Mexico* or something."

"Or *The Seat of the Problem?*" I said, starting to laugh.

"*The Tail End of a Disaster*, you mean," she said, giggling.

Our eyes met for the first time. We just stood there, staring at each other. Then, as if on one of Gerry's best stage cues, we both burst out laughing. We laughed and we laughed until we were crying and laughing at the same time, draped around each other for support.

"Julie," she said at last. "It was dumb to fight. I've really missed you."

"I've missed you, too," I said, "but the fight really wasn't your fault. I know you were only trying to help me. I was stupid and stubborn, and I nearly ended up making a fool of myself."

"But I started it all when I tried to interfere," she said. "No girl likes to find herself on a double date with a guy she hates. I really, genuinely, thought I was doing a nice thing. I thought you would like Phillip and get along great together...you have so much in common. He's even cute."

"I don't hate Phillip," I said. "In fact he's not so bad. But I wanted something better—someone different and exciting. You were right—I want a dream guy. But I think I really have grown up without you around."

"Well, if I promise I won't trick you into another double date as long as we live, can we be friends again?"

"Sure, Gerry," I said. "I've wanted that all along."

"And will you be on the setup committee?"

"I guess so," I said. Then it struck me. "How come you're on it? Don't tell me that the great Geraldine Price hasn't got a date for the formal. I don't believe it. There must be guys in school you haven't dated yet and who would go with you."

"The great Geraldine Price is never without a date,"

she said grandly. "It just happens that my latest boy-friend is a budding socialist. He is only interested in working to improve the Third World masses. He feels that formals are just signs of bourgeois decadence, whatever that means. He says it would betray the poor, starving masses to go out and rent a tux."

"Too cheap to buy a ticket, eh?" I teased.

She started to look annoyed, then she shrugged her shoulders and grinned. "You're probably right. I notice he doesn't think too much about the poor starving masses when we're eating at Al's Bettaburger... Actually, you've made up my mind. I think I'll drop him. I've had enough of buying my clothes at Goodwill. Besides, he's too predictably against conventional things. I don't care about the formal, but it's time to move on to bigger and better things."

"Gerry," I said, smiling at my friend, "when will you realize that boys are not like library books that you pick up and take back when you're tired of them? It's about time you had a good, lasting relationship."

"Oh, I mean to," Gerry said. "As soon as I find the right boy, believe me, I'll stick to him. It would be great, wouldn't it, to have the sort of boy you can share things with, who's always there, who knows how you feel?"

"Great," I agreed, "as long as you can spare a few minutes for your best friend."

"Oh, I'll always do that," Gerry said. "And now you can show me what a best friend you are by helping me get all this paint off my jeans. I still have English and history to get through, so I can't go home and change."

For the next fifteen minutes we scraped and

scrubbed at her jeans until just dull stains were left instead of thick gobs of paint.

"That's the best I can do, I'm afraid," I said, shaking my head as I looked at Gerry's multicolored back. "Those poor jeans are wrecked. I hope they weren't a good pair?"

"One of Tony's Salvation Army shopping sprees, actually," she said. "Seventy-five cents on special."

"Well, you should keep them," I said. "You never know when you may want to date an artist."

"Not me," she said, laughing again. "Never an artist. They are too temperamental. Although Phillip Kaufman doesn't seem temperamental."

"Now, Gerry." I shook my head at her.

"OK," she laughed. "I'm not getting involved."

Chapter Eighteen

GERRY CALLED for me as if nothing had happened, as if the past few weeks had never existed. I was glad to see her again and to be friends with her again, but I knew the past weeks without her had been good for me. During that time I had done all kinds of things on my own, things she wouldn't even believe. I had managed to talk to strangers, to go on dates and to fit in reasonably well with a new set of friends. Even if we went back to being best friends again, I would never be completely in her shadow, waiting for her to find time for me. I probably wasn't going to hang around with Caroline anymore, even if she wanted me, which she wouldn't, but I intended to try new things and maybe to make new friends as well.

Gerry was reading me a list of all the new clothes she wanted.

"You'll just have to get a job if you want to buy yourself so many things," I said, as we crossed our street.

"Me? Get a job? What a horrible idea," she said. "I don't ever intend to get a job. Outside the theater, that is."

"Lots of actresses have to wait tables," I said. "Maybe you should get some experience now."

"Can you see me waiting on other people?" Gerry asked, raising an eyebrow. "You know what I'm like. If someone told me to hurry up, I'd pour the soup all over them. I can't help my terrible temper. If I get a job, I'd have to be boss right away."

"I don't think there are too many jobs like that around," I said. "I'd like to get a job, too, but it would have to be something I like doing!"

Gerry stopped walking and stood there with that excited expression on her face. "Hey, wait a minute!" she said.

"What is it?" I demanded impatiently. Gerry had to dramatize every situation.

"I forgot about it because we weren't speaking last weekend!"

"Forgot about what?"

"That store with the dragons and unicorns! They were advertising for part-time help. That would be a good job for you, and you could probably meet good people there, too."

"No! When did you see it?"

"Last weekend I walked past, and there was a sign in the window!"

"It's probably gone by now."

"Still, you could stop by after school..."

"Yeah, I could do that. Just my luck to hear about a job I would love too late."

"You may not be."

"Now I'll spend all day worrying about it."

"Then cut school and go over this morning."

"Gerry, I'm not the kind of person who cuts school. Besides, the owner wouldn't want to hire the kind of person who cuts school. But I know I'll do terribly on the history test because I'll be thinking about the perfect job I just lost and all the things I can't buy."

As it turned out, I had other things to think about. Caroline cornered me by my locker when I was already pretty late for math.

"Hey, stranger," she said. "We haven't seen you around for a while. Still painting those things for the formal?"

"They're just about finished," I said, shoveling books into my bag.

"I must remember to glance up as we drift by. Then I can say, 'I know the girl who painted those,'" she said, leaning against the next locker. "By the way, I saw the ticket list yesterday, and you aren't on it. Did you forget yesterday was the last day?"

"No," I said, still not meeting her eyes. "I'm not going after all."

"What! You're not going? How come? Have you and what's-his-name broken up?"

This would have been a great moment to tell her that what's-his-name and I were never an item in the first place, apart from ties of kinship. But I wasn't that brave, and she really didn't need to know. Caroline would make sure a story like that was around school in two seconds flat. Although I never really told any lies, this one was mine for keeps.

"I think I told you before," I said. "Danny has finals that week and he can't take the weekend off. His grades are very important to him." That wasn't a lie, so I didn't feel guilty.

"More important than making his girlfriend happy?" Caroline asked. "Some boyfriend. I think you'd be better off without him, Julie. Any boy that doesn't put you first isn't worth having."

I recognized this as another opportunity to rid myself of the Danny myth forever. I could agree to break off with him and who knows, maybe Caroline could get me together with one of her group. Maybe even Gary would ask me out. Then the new, improved Julie Klein, with added brighteners, came through strongly. The Julie Klein that did not have to bend over backwards to make people like her anymore.

"I'm afraid I agree with Danny, Caroline," I said. "I think grades are more important than formals. After all, who will even remember a little freshman dance a few years from now? College grades last forever."

Caroline's large, blue eyes opened very wide, as if I had run down Mom, Apple Pie and the American Way all in one breath. "Well, it's very important to *me*," she said. "And I feel that you've let me down too, Julie. I was counting on Danny being here."

"Oh really? Why?"

She almost blushed. "Oh, I had reasons."

"What reasons?" I demanded.

"I planned to borrow him for a while," she said casually. "I didn't think you'd mind."

"Borrow him?" I asked. It came out as a squeak.

"To make Russ jealous. You understand how it is, don't you? Other girls are always hanging around him, and I can't seem to tell him how much that upsets me.

So I decided to make him annoyed by talking about mature college boys, and then I planned to dance with Danny right under his nose. He would have been so jealous!"

"Well, thanks a lot," I stammered. "Some friend you are! You only wanted me to come so you could steal my date. Did it occur to you how embarrassing it would have been for me to be put through all that?"

"Oh, come on, Julie," she said, pouting like a little girl. "I would have given him back again."

"Nice of you, Caroline," I said frostily. "And if I had been coming, would you have told me about your plan ahead of time?"

"I don't suppose so."

"How mean," I said, gathering up my book bag and starting to walk away. "You never think about how other people feel when you walk all over them. I'm glad I won't be hanging around you anymore, hoping you'll be nice to me."

Then I walked off before she could say anything. As the day wore on, I realized I had made an enemy of the most influential person in our class. But even that didn't seem to be such a life-or-death matter anymore. I had seen through her. Other people would too as they grew up. Being part of the popular crowd didn't really change my life. It just made me change how I thought about myself. Now I didn't need them to think I was OK. I had taken a lot of chances, and I realized I was more my own person than ever. I actually felt good about myself. Maybe that's how Phillip Kaufman felt when he turned Caroline down in eighth grade. I smiled and then got angry. Who cared about Phillip Kaufman anyway?

Chapter Nineteen

WHEN I OPENED the door to Pure Fantasy, the first person I saw, staring at me from behind the counter, was Phillip Kaufman. He looked up and gave me what I took to be a triumphant grin. After my last few days, the date with Steve, the fight with Gerry and the crash with Caroline, I wasn't expecting another encounter.

"Oh no, not you again!" I said with shock in my voice. "Everywhere I go, you are there!"

"I beg your pardon? What have I done to upset you?"

"You've taken my job!"

"I what?"

"This job. I really wanted it. You know I'm crazy about this stuff, and I wanted to work here. I didn't hear about the job until too late, and now you've got it instead." The words all came out in a rush, and I don't think Phillip understood half of them. He looked at me steadily as if I were a dangerous animal and he didn't know what sort of crazy thing I might do next.

Finally he nodded, never taking his eyes from my face. "Oh, I get it. You wanted the job that was advertised here, right?"

"Right," I said, wondering why we always kept being

in the same place or working on the same things.

The ghost of a smile crossed his face. "In that case," he said, "let me give you a little tip. If you want a job you ought to start off by being nice to the owner."

There was a pause while I took this in. Finally I asked hesitantly, "Are you trying to tell me that you are the owner of this place?"

The smile spread. I guess I must have looked pretty silly standing there with my mouth hanging open. "Not exactly," he said. "My mother owns it. But she bought it because she likes to run small stores and is trying to cure me of my strange habits. I believe she felt that if I was surrounded by this fantasy stuff all the time, I might shake off my dreams and start living in the real world. You know, business training instead of dragon slaying. But you could still get the job. It's available. We were just going to put a notice up at the college because we didn't have anyone."

I stared at him. I remembered clearly the woman I had seen in the store when I had been in. Now that I thought about it, he looked exactly like her. "Don't do that. Hire me. But even if you don't," I added hastily, "do you really like all this? You haven't been joking?"

His face lit up as if I had turned on a switch. Phillip's eyes really sparkled. "I'd say it was my passion," he explained. "Somehow I can't ever make today seem as exciting as that world."

"That's how I feel," I blurted out.

"Really?" he said. "I thought so at first, but when I tried to talk to you about it when you were drawing dragons, you said you just liked to draw. And you obviously didn't want to talk to me. I didn't think you'd understand passion. You seemed to be wishy-washy on the subject."

"What?" I said in shock. "Me, wishy-washy? Look who's talking! It's just that most people think it's weird. Honestly, I used to imagine I was a warrior princess in love with a champion dragon slayer. Dumb, huh?"

"Sounds pretty nice to me," he said. "As I told you before, I've always imagined I was the dragon slayer." And he blushed slightly. "I have a terrific collection of dragons—ceramic ones, stuffed ones, glass ones. You must come up and see them sometime."

"Come up and see my dragons. That's a new one," I said, and smiled as the slight blush turned into bright red. "No, I'd really like to see them, Phil. And I'd love to start a collection myself, if I can ever save up enough to afford any of the stuff in this store."

"Well, you'd get a discount if you work here," he said, coming around the counter toward me. I don't have time to run it alone after school, so it would probably be a couple of afternoons a week, and maybe Saturdays."

"Oh wow!" I said. "Do you think I'd get it?"

"I don't know about that," he said with a serious look on his face. "I mean, we can't have emotional outbursts at customers, you know."

"No more emotional outbursts, I promise," I said. "I think I've finally sorted myself out."

A few nights later I was at school, helping to decorate for the Freshman Formal. As Gerry and I came into the gym armed with rolls of paper streamers, thumbtacks, posters and a couple of piñatas, the first person we saw was Phillip Kaufman.

Gerry threw me a worried look. "This wasn't my idea," she said. "I didn't ask him. I swear I didn't even see the names of all the committee members."

"It's OK, Gerry," I said evenly. "I think I can stand to be with him for a couple of hours. In fact, I have a story I've been meaning to tell you."

Phil saw us and came over. "Hey, remember what I was telling you about that fantasy convention? There's one next month. You want me to get tickets to it for us?"

"Oh, great," I beamed. "Yes, I really want to go."

Gerry looked from Phil to me and back again. "Did something happen while I wasn't looking?" she asked.

"Phil's really crazy about fantasy, too," I said, turning to Gerry. "We have a lot in common and we'll probably spend some time together."

"That's what I kept trying to say all along," Gerry said, shaking her head. "If only you'd listened to me in the first place..."

"Oh Gerry, start decorating, will you," I said, taking a poster and climbing the nearest stepladder with it.

Little by little the gym was transformed into a Mexican fiesta. We had a great time hurling across brightly colored streamers to each other, dropping piñatas (one of which exploded, spilling candy in all directions) and generally clowning around. I found I was laughing and clowning as much as anybody.

"Hey, Gerry, how come all the fun people are here?" I asked as we pinned up the last posters together. "Who can be left to go to the formal?"

"All the people who think it matters to be seen at a formal," she said. "But these kids have always been fun. You've just never mixed in before. It looks like you're having a great time. I'd hardly have recognized you as the same person. What made you finally get over your shyness?"

"Oh, I had a bit of practice in the past couple of weeks," I said.

We just got the last traces of our clutter cleared away as the band started to tune up. We left and went out for pizza, hanging around the pizza parlor until midnight, when the formal was over and we were scheduled to clean up. As we came back in through the side door, they were halfway through the last dance, couples swaying mechanically together as they crept around the floor at a snail's pace to a slow, pounding beat. Others sat out around the sides of the floor, staring into space with bored expressions or openly yawning. I looked at all those girls with their stiff, formal hairstyles and their long, elegant dresses and their expensive corsages cascading down in a mass of ribbons, and I remembered how much I had longed to be one of them. But how many of them actually looked as if they were having fun the way we had fun setting up and eating pizza? One girl, sitting near us, had a big, fake smile on her face as if she were trying hard to look happy.

"They all look like patients in a doctor's waiting room," Phillip whispered into my ear.

"That's just what I was thinking," I said. "I'm glad I didn't go after all."

"Did you want to?" he asked, surprised.

"I thought I did. I'm not sour grapes though. I had fun tonight anyway."

"Funny, you never struck me as that sort of girl."

"Oh? What sort of girl did I strike you as?"

"I don't know how to put it in words without saying something I don't mean," he said awkwardly. "You were always so snobby, I guess, and defensive...but I've really enjoyed this evening. Maybe you'll go to the dance next year."

"That's a nice thought," I said.

The last number came to an end. The lights were turned on full again, and the dancers began to gather up their belongings.

"Well, I guess it's back to work," Phil said. "Let's go." As he walked a bit ahead of me, I noticed how his hair curled around his collar in cute little baby curls.

How about that? I asked myself. Who would have thought it? He wasn't any of the things I had dreamed of. He wasn't dark and mature-looking. He didn't make me go limp all over, but I felt comfortable with him. I knew I could be me. That's what I'm ready for. We can be friends right now, and later on, who knows? He might save me from some dragon!

"Hey, look what I've found," Gerry whispered in my ear, showing me a large tray of leftover food, still untouched.

"I don't know how you can think of eating anything," I said. "We must have set a pizza-eating record tonight already."

The last dancers were leaving the room. I recognized Devon, in a beautiful black dress, together with Gary, who looked uncomfortable in a black tux with a frilly shirt. Devon caught sight of me, did a double take and came over.

"Why weren't you here?" she asked. "I saw you a few nights ago with a gorgeous guy at the Last Resort club. What were you doing there? We have trouble getting in. Anyway, I thought you would be bringing him tonight. He was even cuter than the hunk you were with in New York. Where do you manage to find them like that? You're a sly one, Julie Klein. So if you ever have a spare guy, lend him to me... only don't tell Gary. I've got to go. They're waiting for me. See you." She gave me a wink, then ran off to join him.

I turned and saw Gerry standing there with her mouth open.

"Remind me to tell you a very long story," I said as I swept away with a tray of dirty glasses and smiled in her direction.